The Baron and the Mistress
(Revised Edition)
The Rakes of St. Regent's Park #2
By
Karyn Gerrard

I0614803

Table of Contents

The Baron and the Mistress (Revised Edition) 1

Author's Note 2

Rakes of St. Regent's Park Series... 3

Summary.. 4

Dedication and Acknowledgements 5

Prologue.. 6

Chapter 1...12

Chapter 2...23

Chapter 3...31

Chapter 4...36

Chapter 5...43

Chapter 6...52

Chapter 7...60

Chapter 8...70

Chapter 9...76

Chapter 10 85

Chapter 11 97

Chapter 12 104

Chapter 13 111

Chapter 14 118

Chapter 15 126

Chapter 16 137

Chapter 17 145

Chapter 18 153

Chapter 19 161

Chapter 20 167

Chapter 21 172

Epilogue... 184

Author's Note #2 187

Author Biography.. 188

More Books by Karyn Gerrard 189

Sneak Peek of Knight of Christmas.. 191
Prologue.. 192
Chapter 1.. 197

The Baron and the Mistress (Revised Edition)

Copyright © 2015, 2022, by Karyn Gerrard

Vers. 4.2

KG Publishing

(PRINT) ISBN: 978-1-7386845-2-6

Cover art by © Cora Graphics

Author's Note

THE BARON AND THE MISTRESS was published in 2015 as a standalone Victorian historical romance. I decided to revise this to fit The Rakes of St. Regent's Park series, making Asher Colborne, the hero, part of the club. This new revised edition has been expanded and changed enough to warrant a new edition. The basic story remains the same.

I am of the mind that each historical romance author does their own world-building, much like authors in fantasy or other genres. Each author has their own set of characters and peers. That is why many of my characters from other books pop up in the stories I write. They are all part of my particular historical romance world.

Rakes of St. Regent's Park Series

In a private meeting place, in an old bank office behind Colosseum Terrace on Albany Street, a group of gentlemen attended a gathering. It had nothing to do whatsoever with financing, investments, or stocks—unless you counted moral bankruptcy. The central rules of this club: no serious attachments to anyone, and the pursuit of one's own pleasures, especially of the carnal variety, were to be of the utmost importance.

But weariness and boredom were setting in. Along with something more worrying: loneliness. A disquiet of the soul. These bad-boy peers of Victorian London were damaged, hiding their inner torture beneath a thin veneer of devil-may-care dissoluteness.

It takes an exceptional group of women to capture the hearts of such men. To see past the outer shell. The ladies are determined to live and love in their own way, with no relinquishment of their independence and no compromises. How satisfying to find that deep down, these progressive men are in total agreement.

Summary

A SHIVERING YOUNG WOMAN leans against a lamppost on London's most notorious street of ill repute.

Chastity Armitage is on the run from her lecherous stepfather. Desperate for food and lodging for her siblings, she takes to the streets. She never expected a tall, handsome man to appear from the mist and change her life forever. A choice lies before her: continue down the path of never-ending poverty or become the baron's mistress.

Asher Colborne, Baron Wenlock, is shocked to discover the dressed-in-rags lady is Chastity Armitage, a young woman who had caught his attention at a ball three years past. Asher offers his assistance, but Chastity suggests a carnal contract. As a member of The Rakes of St. Regent's Park, Asher is well aware of what such an agreement will portend.

Despite the scorching attraction, they decide to keep an emotionless business arrangement in place. That pact soon falls apart, as they cannot deny their intense feelings. Many obstacles lay in Chastity and Asher's path. For the baron and the mistress, embracing true love will be their most challenging impediment.

Dedication and Acknowledgements

To my live-in hero, who encourages me every step of the way in my publishing journey. Thank you, as always.

Big thanks to Cora Graphics for the beautiful cover.

Prologue

LONDON, ENGLAND
November 1897

If there was one thing the Rakes of St. Regent's Park understood, it was how to have a rousing good time.

Asher Colborne, Baron Wenlock, was out on the town with his fellow rakes.

He sat at a table with the remaining members of their private association. Over the past fifteen years, the membership had ebbed and flowed. Some went to war, others married, and they moved on to a less profligate life. Part of the current group had formed a close bond in school, all the way to Cambridge University until today.

Not just anyone was allowed within this privileged circle. First and foremost, the other members had to genuinely like the fellow, and these formidable men did not give their friendship or trust or readily reveal their emotions.

The recently engaged Christian Bamford, Duke of Allenby and former group leader, attended tonight as a farewell. Not only was he leaving their club, but they had gathered to also say their goodbyes to Brandon Knight, who would depart for Herne Bay in a couple of weeks.

Much had happened with the Rakes of St. Regent's Park. One could argue that their organization neared its end. At its peak, there were twenty-one members.

Recently, they were down to seven.

Now? Their numbers were about to deplete even further.

It was rather depressing when Asher thought about it. He had recently made an invitation to Oliver Wollstonecraft, grandson to Aidan Wollstonecraft, Earl of Carnstone. The twenty-six-year-old heir to the earl had earned a bit of a notorious reputation that came close to his grandfather Aidan's scandalous younger years in the 1840s. Or so the rumors claimed.

Oliver had said he would think it over, but that was weeks ago. All of the other members had yet to bother with recruitment. Even Asher's pursuit of Oliver had been half-hearted.

Asher glanced around the table at his friends and fellow members. Sitting next to him was the elder statesman, as they called him, Gideon Broyles, Duke of Watford, the last original founding member. About to turn forty, Gideon outpaced them all for casual liaisons. He showed no signs of slowing down or settling down.

Warren Cowley, Viscount Huxley, was making a rare appearance, as he had been tucked away at the Bevan Sanitorium in Hertfordshire, receiving treatment for his sexual excesses. Huxley arrived in London this week to attend to business.

Asher had been shocked at the change in the man, as Huxley was more withdrawn than ever. He sat, nursing a scotch, barely speaking.

Next to Huxley was Damon Cranston, Marquess of Brookton and heir to The Duke of Chellenham. Damon would be taking over as the leader of their little clique.

Damon's scandalous stature was the talk of London. Society referred to the dashing marquess as the fictional Oscar Wilde character Dorian Gray. But Asher had wondered through the years—how much of the gossip was accurate?

Merritt Redfern, Viscount Tolwood and heir to the Earl of Shelton, was not a full-blown member of their group but more of an apprentice—until he found a suitable bride. Brookton called Tolwood their eager puppy mascot.

By the end of the year, it could only be Asher, Gideon, and Damon left. Not that any of them were active rakes at the moment, for Asher had the distinct impression most of the dalliances were all talk, complete fiction. If the men could agree on anything, it would be the tedium of their lives and the utter boredom surrounding their indolent elite existence. If they ever decided to be honest about anything, including feelings.

"I say, allowing your soon-to-be duchess to keep her investigative agency? Christian, you are progressive to the core," Merritt said, raising his glass. "I salute you."

Christian's fiancée owned and operated a successful investigative firm, The Galway Agency, with her sister and cousin.

"Thank you. As if I could dictate to Eleanora what to do, not that I would. The Galway Investigative Agency will go on. The private detective business has been brisk. At some point, she may reduce her hours. But that will be *her* decision."

Christian reached for the decanter and freshened his drink. "Let's face facts, lads. A new century yawns before us. Do you think those of us with titles and societal standing will even factor into shaping the future? Our way of life is near its end."

"Bite your tongue," Damon scoffed. "There will always be a peerage."

"Perhaps, but the power our grandfathers and great-grandfathers wielded at the turn of this century? Gone forever. Good riddance, I say," Christian replied.

"How goes the bride search, Tolwood?" Gideon asked, his tone of voice showing that he wasn't interested in knowing. He had changed the subject because the truth of their future wasn't something Gideon wished to discuss, let alone accept.

Asher understood completely.

Merritt sighed. "Still going. Finding someone to love and who will love you in return is blasted difficult. I may have to settle for an alliance."

"Why marry at all?" Brandon interjected. "We're supposed to be scandalous rakes."

Knight was a wealthy businessman of the gentry class. Gideon had sponsored Knight, and they all accepted him into the club. He was not an easy man to get to know, but, Asher supposed, all the men had barriers of one form or another around them for whatever reasons. Brandon Knight was the only non-peer in the current group.

Back to the current conversation, it was true what Brandon said. They were *supposed* to be rakes. But, as Asher surmised before, he doubted many of them still embraced such an existence or even lived it to the full.

They all had their various predilections when it came to carnal pleasures. Gideon? He frequented clubs that offered light birching. Damon? Orgies were his preference. Warren? Well, he had gone too far and sought treatment for his dissipation. Warren sought out multiple sexual encounters beyond the norm.

As for Asher?

He found pleasure in the East End, with anonymous sex in the various back alleys. Oh, he was careful, as were all the rakes. He used protection. Why he sought out sex in such grubby circumstances, he could not say. Be damned if he would try and puzzle it out here.

"The way things are going," Gideon said, his deep voice rumbling. "We will have to recruit new members."

"Yes, we have discussed this before. I invited Oliver Wollstonecraft, although he hasn't gotten back to me," Asher interjected. "He's the heir apparent to the Earl of Carnstone. I will broach the subject with him again."

"Why even bother expanding the membership?" Christian stated. "Marriage may not be as horrible as you may think."

"Please spare us your cloying happiness," Damon replied in a dull voice. "Just because you were caught in a marriage trap doesn't mean the rest of us wish it. Except for Tolwood."

"And what of Althea?" Christian replied softly.

"What's this?" Asher exclaimed, his interest piqued. Althea Galway was Eleanora's younger sister and partner in the investigative agency. When had Damon shown any interest in a woman beyond his meaningless encounters?

Never.

Damon flushed.

An actual reaction. Now, *this* was interesting.

"She means nothing to me. I wouldn't give a care if I ever saw her again." Damon threw back the rest of his drink and refilled his glass.

He was lying, and all the men in the room knew it.

"Just as well," Christian replied. "She has said the same of you. Which proves that you both lie."

Damon flushed further, his jaw working furiously.

Christian was correct. Could something develop there?

Perhaps not, knowing Damon's stubborn and dissipated nature.

"So, when are you leaving exactly, Knight?" Warren asked. It was the first time he had spoken in over an hour.

"December fifteenth," Brandon replied.

"Out for revenge regarding past hurts, correct?" Warren threw back his drink. "Take care, do not allow it to consume your life."

"Too late," Brandon replied, his voice firm. "It already has."

Asher downed the rest of his scotch and stood. Enough of this insipid conversation. They were talking in circles. "Shall we partake in a game of cards? There is a private room in the rear. There is also a small buffet set up." He motioned toward the door.

"I say, I am famished," Merritt said.

"Christian? Stay and play. You're not under a self-imposed curfew, I trust?" Asher teased good-naturedly.

"Not at all. Cards it is. I hope roast beef is available," Christian replied, rubbing his hands together. "And duchess potatoes."

"I made certain to order it," Asher replied with a grin. "I ensured all your favorites, including Charlotte russe for dessert, are on the menu. And as an extra surprise, Eleanora sent apple scones."

Christian laid his hand on Asher's shoulder and squeezed it affectionately. "You are a true friend."

Everyone stood and headed toward the back room.

Except for Warren.

Asher stayed behind. His friend was not well, physically or emotionally. The look of desolation on Warren's face concerned Asher. He had worried about his friend and thought of him often these past weeks he was away.

"What is it? What's going on?" Asher asked, his voice quiet.

"I am returning to the sanitorium. I have relapsed already. Speaking of consuming one's life, I'm a hopeless case and should be shut away permanently." Warren's voice was agitated, his first show of emotion in a long time.

Asher shook his head. "I *am* sorry, my friend. Is there anything I can do?"

"There is one thing you can do for me. Leave this group, Ash. Stop seeking out thrills in the back alleys. Find someone to love. Although, I am aware it is not an easy task in this cold world. This existence is pathetic and soul-destroying. Be done with it before you turn into an empty, rotting husk like me. Or Gideon or Brandon. Damon is more than halfway there. Take my advice and save yourself."

Warren headed to the private room, leaving Asher shaken.

The stark warning had taken root.

Chapter 1

LONDON, ENGLAND
  Early December 1897

Chastity Armitage's given name could be construed as ironic, considering she was looking for a quick shilling tup in Shag Alley. Of course, that wasn't the actual name of the darkened, dead-end street. Prostitutes plied their wares there, and customers from all walks of life and social standings sampled and paid for such wares, which explained the silly name. It was somewhat laughable when one thought about it.

But nothing about Chastity's life was laughable. Not at all.

Trembling from the cold, Chastity gripped the nearby lamppost to steady her shaky legs. In truth, she wasn't a prostitute in the strictest sense of the word—just a desperate young woman. Or so she told herself when the horrid memories haunted her troubled dreams on a near-nightly basis.

A thick fog rolled down the lane, covering its broken cobbles with ugly swirls of color. The pungent aroma of unburned street lamp gas filled the air and mixed with the odor of raw sewage. It blended with the sound of rutting sex from the alleyway.

Chastity gagged and brought her tattered sleeve to her nose for relief.

Two months ago, she lost her virginity to a rough laborer in this notorious alley—it had been an absolute necessity. The act—done against the brick wall and mercifully swift—resulted in a few coins thrown at her feet. That money kept her younger brother and sister from starving and immediate eviction.

However, the paltry funds were almost gone. It is why Chastity was seeking a paying customer. The rent was overdue, and they had no food. Things could not be any direr. Every day was a constant struggle to keep a roof over her family's head and a crust of bread on the table. What would she do once winter arrived in full force? Thankfully, it had been warmer than usual for early December. But how long would the weather stay amenable? Once conditions took a turn, they would need fuel for a fire.

How had everything gone so wrong?

A trail of unfortunate events led her to this exact place and time. Where to begin her wretched tale?

Her father's death and her mother's rapid—and it had turned out, necessary—remarriage—her mother's sudden illness and passing.

Then—the escape.

A carriage rattled by, splashing mud on her already dirty wool skirt. Two men staggered toward her, making lewd comments as they passed a whisky bottle back and forth between them. Chastity looked away and exhaled in utter weariness.

Please let them keep walking by.

They were drunk, and she instinctively knew they would be rough and cruel. After all, it had been the totality of her experience with men, save her poor father. She exhaled in relief as they stumbled down the lane, more interested in the bottle than her. Blocking out the foul sights and odors swirling around her, she focused instead on her current predicament.

Chastity and her siblings, Jon and Hannah, had fled their home in the most urgent and dire circumstances. It was hard to believe that over two years had passed since that fateful night. It seemed longer. Since then, she had agonized over the quick escape, wondering if she'd made the correct decision.

The reason for the sudden departure? Their mother had died five days before that hasty getaway. They were left in the care of their stepfather, Sir Nigel Barrington, who made no secret of his deviant plans for them.

Chastity pulled her tattered shawl around her shoulders and shuddered, touching the bare spot at her throat as a few hot tears clustered on her eyelashes. Blinking them away, she frowned. There was no time to wallow in self-indulgent tears. Feeling sorry for herself was not a luxury she could afford, not when there were many pressing problems.

Yet, her thoughts drifted to the past again. It still was. Shielding then-eleven-year-old Jon and eight-year-old Hannah had become Chastity's primary focus.

Protecting Jon in particular.

She'd witnessed the lustful looks cast Jon's way.

Memories of the night Barrington had skulked into her brother's bedroom flooded her mind. Thank God she had beaten the horrid man off with a copper warming pan. They had escaped that night with not much more than the clothes on their backs, and sadly, they had no family or close friends to assist. Luckily, she sold the gold cross that had hung about her neck for the much-needed coin.

Once sold, the small diamond necklace had kept them fed and housed for many weeks—with proper and prudent budgeting. The jewelry had been a gift for her twelfth birthday, and she hated to part with it.

Since then, Jon managed to make a few farthings doing odd jobs about the streets, and Hannah sporadically worked for a ragpicker. These low-paying, temporary positions weren't enough to keep the wolf from the door.

The workhouse beckoned.

Sniffling, Chastity wiped away a wayward tear. They would be separated at the workhouse, which is why she hadn't taken them there in the first place. It would be the first logical place to search. The looming specter of Barrington finding them had also fueled her decision.

However, the evil man almost certainly didn't care where they were or what became of them. While their mother was alive, his rank indifference spoke of the depth of his disdain. But when her mother passed, that last barrier crashed down. The change in the man had not been subtle.

At first, he plied them with kindness and extra sweets. He started touching them, little caresses of affection that were not the least bit innocent. Then Barrington cast his lascivious gaze toward Jon, who was considered the best-looking of the siblings. Jon would grow into a handsome man; all the signs were plain to see.

Barrington would stroke Jon's cheek, whispering how beautiful he was.

It'd been enough to turn her bile. One particular incident fueled her worst fears. Barrington, after they had completed dinner, pulled Jon into his lap. The special attention that he'd paid her brother made her skin crawl. Chastity, not very experienced in the ways of men, instinctively understood the leering, salacious look Sir Nigel gave Jon.

A strange, disturbing light gleamed in his eye while stroking Jon's back with his claw-like hand. When Jon had told her later that night, he'd felt something growing hard in their stepfather's lap; she understood then that they might have to make a hasty departure.

Never had she believed it would happen so soon.

A girl at school once told her of a man's *thing* and how he could stick it in you and make a baby. She later surmised the "thing" could be shoved into any opening—boy or girl. No one would harm her siblings if Chastity had anything to say about it.

Since then, she had learned the vulgar words used for that part of a man:

Cock. Prick. Willy. Tackle. Whore-pipe.

Straightening her shoulders, she glanced about the dingy street. Enough. As she surmised earlier, there was no time to wallow in the past and lament their fates. Today is all she must focus on. Her resolve quickened and hardened into sword steel. She must make money to ward off that slimy toad of a landlord. He had leeringly suggested that she work off the back rent.

Chastity preferred a swift rut in Shag Alley before allowing that ghastly man with rotten teeth and smelling of dead fish to lay a hand on her. Once she succumbed to his demands, he would never leave her alone.

Virtue and pride be damned, protecting her siblings overrode everything.

Everything.

ASHER COLBORNE HAD a successful night of gaming at one of his favorite haunts. Sitting in the carriage with Oliver Wollstonecraft, he counted the pound notes.

"How much did you win?" Oliver asked.

"I came out ahead, just barely, so I call it successful."

Oliver laughed. "Better than me; I'm down thirty pounds. I am feeling lucky. Where to next? My fortunes are about to turn; I can feel it."

After a victorious night of cards, Asher usually sought a quick rut in the infamous Shag Alley. But ever since his last meeting with his fellow rakes, he had yet to go anywhere for a hard and fast tup.

He wasn't sure what he would do instead.

Luck was certainly on his side tonight.

Go to another club for more games of chance, perhaps? Or he could confound the Gods, head home, and make an early night of it. Reading by the fire with a snifter of brandy sounded more appealing by the moment. He had books aplenty to choose from. Asher had been staying in more often since Warren's passionate plea for him to give up his decadent life. Warren's wearily urgent words had played over in Asher's mind since.

"I think I've had enough for tonight, but I can drop you anywhere you wish," Asher replied.

"Perhaps The Chrysalis. I fancy a quick tumble with a beautiful woman."

"You may wish to seek another brothel," Asher interjected. "I have it on good authority that they are not careful concerning certain practices. You don't want the pox."

"Hell. Thanks for the warning," Oliver murmured.

"If you joined The Rakes of St. Regent Park, you would be privy to information in this vein."

"Yes, you mentioned your club before."

"Despite the name and the reputation, there are good men in the assembly. We could use more good men, such as yourself. Your family has a sterling reputation for good works. Perhaps that is something the club should aspire to. Something worthwhile, beyond our dissipated indulgences."

Oliver cocked an eyebrow. "Who are you, and what have you done with Wenlock?"

Asher chuckled, then sobered. "I have been doing a little self-examining as of late. I believe some changes are warranted for the club and my personal doings. You don't have to start as a full-fledged member. Join as a prospect, and see if the club is a good fit for you."

Oliver slipped on his leather gloves. "Perhaps I will. I suppose there are fees."

"Only a small pittance to keep the place stocked with liquor and food. What will your family say about your joining, that is, if you decide to do so?"

Oliver shrugged. "I am twenty-six years of age; they have no say over my life. It will be decades before I am Earl of Carnstone. My father is before me, and the men in my family have long lifelines. I am happy to say that my grandfather, the current earl, is full of health and vitality. I intend to enjoy my freedom."

"Well said. Regardless, do give it serious thought. How about I drop you at Mollie's in the East End?"

"Yes, thank you."

Asher tapped twice on the ceiling, and the small window slid open. "To Mollie's, Andrews."

"Yes, my lord," his driver replied.

After saying goodnight to Oliver, Asher pounded on the roof. It lurched forward. Pulling aside the curtain, he glanced outside and could swear he saw Oliver striding in the opposite direction, away from the brothel. How strange. Maybe he changed his mind.

Asher's thoughts turned reflective as he headed home. Recently turned thirty, Asher wondered if it was time to take stock of his life. He should do as Warren has done, cloister himself away in the country to rest and reflect.

But Warren had more significant issues to consider. It wasn't only weariness. His friend had a sickness or disease, like anyone who overindulged in alcohol or drugs.

A loss of control.

Would that be the fate of all in The Rakes of St. Regent's Park group?

Asher certainly didn't wish it to be *his* future.

Moving aside the curtain with his walking stick, he glanced out at the street. His driver took a circuitous route through the East End toward a few of Asher's preferred areas. Best let Andrews know he would return home instead of indulging in anonymous sex.

But before he could, his eyes were drawn to a figure leaning against a street lamp.

A young woman, all but swallowed up by the swirling fog.

An attractive young woman.

His eyes widened in recognition.

No. It could not possibly be her.

His heart leaped in his chest at the possibility. Every nerve ending sparked to life, tingling his skin.

"Stop the carriage!" Asher yelled as he banged his walking stick on the roof. He couldn't believe it; he must investigate this. He had to know.

What the bloody hell is she doing, loitering about Shag Alley?

The distant but never forgotten memories flickered through his mind. A ball at the Earl of Dunham's posh estate more than two years past is where he'd first seen her. Actually, it was closer to three years ago, but no matter.

Chastity—Armitage.

Yes, that was her name.

It had been infatuation at first sight, at least on his end. The young woman's luminescent beauty had lit up the entire ballroom. Wearing a cranberry-colored silk frock that complimented her exquisitely styled golden-brown hair, how could his gaze not be drawn to her? The gown caressed lush curves, giving him an impressive cockstand for most of the night.

Chastity Armitage possessed the face of an innocent angel, but he'd also seen the teasing gleam in her eye and the animation in her varied expressions. The young lady would be passionate in bed; Asher would have wagered on it.

Lively and attractive, yet she hadn't acted like the rest of the giggling and simpering misses. A quiet intelligence and dignity had radiated from her. He'd been utterly and completely captivated. By the supper dance, his feelings encompassed far more than physical yearnings.

Unfortunately, Chastity departed the ball before he secured a formal introduction. Two weeks later, Asher convinced his father to broach the subject with Sir Nigel Barrington, her stepfather and legal guardian. Barrington had been knighted recently for one thing or another. He couldn't recall for what, but it was no doubt the reason for the man's appearance at the exclusive ball.

The crushing disappointment in learning that Chastity had permanently relocated to a remote part of Northern Scotland with her younger brother and sister had stayed with him for months.

Eventually, the girl faded from recent memory into the mist of dreams.

The recollections came roaring back now, along with complicated emotions Asher couldn't, or wouldn't, name.

He focused on the young lady leaning against the lamppost. It was hard to reconcile that they were the same person. If this slender stalk of a female turned out to be Chastity Armitage, she was a good deal thinner and dressed in a ghastly manner.

He had to know one way or the other.

Asher opened the carriage door and stepped down, not waiting for the driver's assistance. He was familiar with Shag Alley, like most young men in his social circle. He had no trouble navigating the crowded, dim street. As Asher moved closer, the young woman glanced at him with wide greenish-brown eyes.

Damn, it is her!

Masking his surprise, Asher stopped in front of her. Those beautiful eyes flashed a brief show of fear. But what struck him was the profundity of fatigue and misery swimming in their depths. The vital, sparkling girl he'd fallen instantly for at the ball—no longer existed.

My God, what has she been through?

His gaze roved over her shivering, dressed-in-rags frame. Even though Chastity appeared slight, her curves were still apparent enough to send a flare of desire straight to his thickening shaft. Damn his rampant libido. This reaction was not appropriate at all under the circumstances.

But more than a physical reaction, he wanted to protect her from all that would harm her. Hold her close, allowing no one to cause her any pain. But it looked as though she had experienced her share already, and that horrible thought arrowed straight to his heart, causing it to spasm with grief.

"Quick tup, guv'nor?"

Perhaps it *wasn't* her.

Those were the last words he would have expected to pass Chastity Armitage's lips.

Asher's eyes narrowed in suspicion. Her working-class accent sounded counterfeit, and her pale skin did not show a lifetime of strife and poverty. The lassitude looked to be of a more recent development. Playing along with her performance would be best until he gathered more information.

"Nothing I do is quick, my sweet. I wish to hire you for the entire night. Shall we say—fifteen shillings?" He kept his voice emotionless, though it was a struggle.

Her jaw dropped open briefly; then, she swiftly hid her surprise.

Asher offered what amounted to a week's salary for most laborers. He must have stunned the young woman, for she remained silent.

"Not in the alley," he continued in a disinterested tone. "I will secure us a room. First, I believe; we shall eat. Come." Asher extended his gloved hand toward her.

Chastity stared at it, then her gaze swept over his form, lingering on his formal attire.

Shaking her head, she turned away. "Leave me alone."

Ah.

The accent was a sham as she answered him in perfectly concise and educated English. Asher reached for her hand and pulled her toward the waiting coach.

By God, he would obtain answers to his questions.

Considering that a roll of heat swiftly traveled through him when he clasped her hand, there was no denying that he still wanted her.

I still desired her.

As he had with no other young woman before—or since.

Chapter 2

CHASTITY ALLOWED THE well-dressed gentleman to take her away in his carriage. It was not prudent, but Chastity was desperate enough to see this through to its inevitable conclusion. They had not gone far or spoken during the short journey. They now sat in a private room at The Pig and Whistle Tavern.

Her stomach rumbled. The man, who had introduced himself as Ash, insisting that she call him by that name, ordered beef stew, ale, and extra bread and cheese.

Fifteen shillings?

The obscene amount still rattled about in her bewildered brain. It was the only reason she came with this man. It was a veritable windfall. The money would keep her—and her brother and sister—comfortable for weeks if she budgeted wisely. They could pay the rent owed. Buy firewood, a cake of soap, meat pies, cheese, some apples and potatoes, a new blanket that was not threadbare—the list was endless!

Chastity fought to keep her exhilaration under wraps. It would be prudent not to expose how desperately she required the money, though one look at her attire spoke truth to her visible despair. Honestly, she looked a sight.

What in God's name did he wish to do with her? Or *to* her? What perverse act would she be subjected to? His intense stare made her uncomfortable.

This Ash was too handsome by far.

After removing his hat and gloves, he ran his hand through his black-as-midnight hair. His eyes were the color of a fine cognac, and the patent interest that shone from them sent waves of heat through her. That swift reaction stunned her. How inappropriate.

One must never find a customer attractive. Or so she had heard. And that precisely is who he was, a paying customer, nothing more. Chastity would do well to remember it.

Turning her attention to this Ash, she observed that the silver lining of his cloak was made of the finest silk. His tall frame was perfectly proportioned, and how well he filled out the excellently tailored evening wear. A smartly tied silver cravat completed the fashion, and he looked every inch the rake. Chastity caught a whiff of expensive cologne. The scent of bergamot and lemon invaded her senses. Her stomach dipped precipitously.

Dear heaven, I find him attractive. This is not wise. Not at all.

Chastity's gaze darted about the small room, trying to find a hasty escape route. She found it was always prudent to do so in any situation. Living on the streets had taught Chastity many hard lessons.

"What is your name, my sweet?" he asked, giving her a heated look.

His voice was cultured. The sensual baritone was as rich as melted dark chocolate.

Should she give her real name? What would it matter at this point? "Chastity."

The man's eyes widened as he shifted in his seat, but his concentrated gaze never wavered. "Interesting choice of name for a prossie," the man murmured.

Fury boiled in her veins. "I'm not a-a prossie!"

The corner of his mouth quirked. "Of course not, even though you offered me a quick tup—for coin."

Chastity's cheeks burned with humiliation. The man was correct. How to explain? Why explain it at all, it was not this Ash's business, and she should tell him so. Before she could answer, the barmaid entered the room carrying a tray of foodstuffs. The tantalizing aroma of beef, grilled onions, and fresh bread made her salivate.

For a meal and fifteen shillings, she would agree to anything.

Anything at all.

And she would wager that this arrogant, handsome man knew it.

CHASTITY PULLED A TATTERED rag from her sleeve, snatched pieces of bread and cheese, wrapped the cloth around them, and then set the bundle in her lap. Reaching for the spoon, she stole a glance at Asher. He kept his gaze firm on her, trying his keep his wayward and intensifying emotions under wraps.

Starving, she barely swallowed the stew before shoving in another portion. Realizing she had revealed too much, especially her ravenous hunger, she slowly buttered her bread. Her half-remembered table manners amused but also saddened him.

There were so many questions, but Asher could not speak them aloud. Not yet. His heart hitched in his chest, for the emotions tearing through him were confounding indeed.

Empathy. Desire. Compassion. Passion.

He could not allow himself to succumb to *any* of them. He had only experienced this sort of emotional turmoil once—when he first saw Chastity at the earl's ball. And he had not experienced them since, until tonight.

Asher had one purpose for bringing her here: to discover what happened and how she had come to such circumstances. He genuinely wished to know. Asher could assist her in some altruistic way. If he believed The Rakes should be doing more to help the less fortunate, this could be an excellent place to start.

However, if he lived up to his rake reputation, he could fulfill all his fantasies concerning Chastity Armitage. After all, she was a prostitute.

She was undoubtedly well-versed in pleasing a man and had done it many times. To her, he'd be nothing more than another customer.

Asher's arousal twitched in response, thoroughly agreeing with his assessment. Since they were never properly introduced, they could share a tumble in the sheets, part ways, and he need never think of her again. But he had realized relatively recently that he was not that disreputable rake deep down, not when it counted. And certainly not in this situation.

He was deluding himself on one matter: he had never entirely forgotten her.

More than anything, he wanted to know about her situation. It would be best to keep his focal point on that purpose and dismiss the distracting and intense feelings roiling deep inside.

"I have rented the room above for the night," he declared, playing the part of the arrogant, wealthy customer.

The spoon halted before her luscious mouth. Even observing her eat sent waves of desire cascading through Asher.

Chastity laid the spoon on the table. "I would rather get on with it, then. The sooner it's over with, the sooner I can leave."

Well, that slew my erection.

"You're hungry; I would suggest that you eat. You will need the strength for what lies ahead," Asher said. Rather a braggart statement, but suitable for the role that he played.

Chastity met his gaze, her chin raised. "And what, pray to tell, lies ahead?"

Asher leaned forward. "I intend to fuck you. You will enjoy it, I assure you."

Asher didn't speak this way as a rule; he did it more to elicit a reaction from her. Chastity shrugged with indifference. Nor did she flinch at his vulgar and egotistical declaration, so much for any emotional response.

"Seeing it only happened twice, and the second time the man did not even stick it in me; what you said means nothing." Chastity continued with her meal.

Twice? Only twice?

An uneasiness moved through him. Asher's conscience reared its insistent head. His assumption of vast sexual experience on her part was incorrect, but what else was he to think, considering she propositioned him? It proves that baseless suppositions were constantly occurring within his class, and he was just as guilty of it as those snobby elites he often disdained. He reached for the ale and drank half of the beverage in one gulp.

Chastity stood. "I'm ready."

She acted as if she were headed to the guillotine. Might as well take her to the room, Asher had rented it for the entire night, and he could offer it to her if she had no place to stay. But first, he wanted to continue this conversation in a more private setting, which was his original intent.

He glanced into the near-empty bowl while reaching for his hat and cloak. "Very well, come with me."

Once he unlocked the upstairs room, Asher stepped inside. The interior of the room had certainly seen better days. Various layers of wallpaper were visible on the walls. The ceiling paint had peeled, and water dripped under the worn wood beams.

Asher pulled back the blanket on the bed and recoiled. With a shudder of disgust, he tore off the dirty, threadbare sheets and tossed them to the floor. Asher could locate better accommodations than this. Once they had their conversation, he would find a suitable inn.

And then what?

As he turned to face Chastity, she sunk to her knees. Nimbly, she unfastened the fall of his trousers, reached in, and closed her fist around his erect prick.

Asher's breath seized in his chest, and all rational thought and verbosity fled. Blood coursed to his head, causing the room to spin, and it rushed to his cock, hardening it further.

"I've never done this before, but I've seen the act performed often in the alley. Some men seem to like it," she murmured.

Like it? I bloody well love it.

No words could describe the sensation of a woman's warm mouth closing about his prick. Asher tried to say something—anything—but he could not speak. It was as if he froze into inaction.

Chastity gripped him tight and rolled her hand up and down his shaft. Then she looked up at him with a frank gaze. "You do want this?"

Asher could not form words; all he could do was nod vigorously. All sense fled from him; he couldn't think straight. Decency bade him to stop this before it went any further since his conscience continued to wrestle with his lust for dominance. But it all happened so fast that his brain lost the ability to do anything but surrender.

Once she pulled his erection out of his trousers, she continued exploring, stroking him, running her tongue along his length.

This is most decidedly *not* what he had brought her to this room for. But when her mouth closed over the head of his cock, all remaining rational thought left him.

Decency concedes defeat.

Her innocent sucking nearly made him come right then. Chastity soon found a sensual rhythm by twisting the base of his aching erection as she took him deep into her mouth.

Asher rocked his hips forward. His bollocks tightened, and the pressure built. How many times had he dreamt of Chastity doing this very thing? Again, Asher tried to speak, but all that left his throat were lascivious groans of desire.

I must stop this.

But he couldn't. Asher's selfish desires had taken complete control. Chastity moved faster.

"Wait—" he managed to croak.

Too late.

His peak hit him hard, causing his vision to swirl. Black dots swam in his eyes as his knees buckled. Asher grasped the wall to keep from losing his balance. How could he describe the sensations rolling through him? In all his sexual escapades, he'd never climaxed with this intensity.

Chastity stood and wiped her mouth with her sleeve. She began to unbutton her worn clothing.

"Wait—"

Was that all he could say? What in hell *could* he say after that? With trembling hands, he tucked himself into his trousers, pushed from the wall, and on shaking legs, headed toward her.

"You do not have to do anymore. I never thought—" Asher reached in his pocket, pulled out some of his winnings, close to eight pounds, and thrust the notes into her hand. "Take it. Take it all."

Myriad and confusing emotions gripped him. Emotions he could not name.

Nor did he want to, not here and now.

Asher kissed her hard. He thrust his tongue deep, leaving no part of her lush mouth untouched.

At first, Chastity did not respond. Then the money fluttered to the floor as her thin arms encircled his neck, and she returned his passionate kiss with the desire he instinctively knew lurked within her.

Groaning, he cupped her backside through the tattered woolen skirt. The battle began afresh between desire and decorum. Chastity tasted sweet, and the kiss seared heat throughout his body. He delved deeper, exploring every part of her mouth. Chastity wrapped her tongue around his, caressing and stroking. Asher pulled her closer, his insides aflame. The kiss reached a part of him he had no idea existed. Asher's wayward emotions moved beyond passion, and the realization made him step back.

My wits have gone a-begging.

This inappropriate dalliance could not continue.

She had utterly unmanned him.

The kiss was devastating in its depth and meaning. But hang it all if Asher would examine it tonight. It was best to see Chastity on her way. Forget this ever happened. He reached down, grabbed the pound notes, then handed them to her. Chastity blinked, looking as confused as he felt.

Asher pointed to the door. "Come with me. I will escort you to your lodgings if you have any. Otherwise, you are welcome to use the room for the night, or I can find you better accommodations."

"I have lodgings."

Once they reached the ground floor, Asher hailed the barmaid. He whispered instructions in her ear, and she returned with a small bundle within minutes. Ash slipped a coin into the maid's hand, nodding his thanks.

Facing Chastity, he handed the food to her. "More bread and cheese. Let us depart."

Asher took her arm and escorted her out of the tavern. Why had he impulsively purchased food?

Guilt? Pity? Kindness?

Yes. Chastity Armitage was causing a maelstrom within him, and it unnerved him. It was best to see her home and forget this.

And in his confusion, he had forgotten to ask about her circumstances, so eager he was to put this situation from his mind. Asher should never have instigated this encounter. All it did was turn his world on its axis. And that kind of upheaval he did not need.

Yet, why did he experience a sense of sadness at their upcoming parting? And a sense of loss at what could have been.

Chapter 3

CHASTITY FOLLOWED ASH to the waiting carriage with the money safely tucked away in her battered reticule and the knotted cloths of bread and cheese tightly clenched in her hand.

Why was this Ash accompanying her? She couldn't reveal the address, for she did not want him to know where she lived. Not only was she embarrassed at the address of the run-down accommodations, but it was also best for safety reasons.

And why did this wealthy man cut their encounter short? Chastity would have stayed and done anything he wanted.

His kiss had tasted heavenly but also hinted at the devil within. Shock and desire still reverberated deep inside from her wicked act. What possessed her to take that masculine part of him into her mouth? Her cheeks flushed with the realization that she liked it more than she thought she might.

Chastity placed those thoughts behind her and began formulating a plan for the future. With this money, they could move to better quarters. Perhaps a boarding house with more than a dirty room with cracked plaster walls and broken window glass. Nothing fancy but an establishment with a more permanent and respectable address. They could find long-term employment. Hope took root in her numbed and damaged soul for the first time in two years.

After assisting her into the carriage, Ash took the seat opposite. The window slid open. The coachman peered in, causing Chastity to jump.

"Where to, my lord?" the man asked.

Lord?

That meant this Ash held the title of baron, viscount, or earl. Or he could be the second son of a duke and even the third or fourth. The way that he dressed should have clued her to his exalted status. How mortifying. But it also explained his generous payment. These handful of pound notes were no doubt mere pocket change to him. But this money was everything to Chastity. It meant survival, at least for the short term.

Ash was a member of the peerage. Out of her class then and most definitely in the here and now. Their social connection would be unlikely even if she still lived with her stepfather.

Good heavens, as if this man would pay court to her after what she'd done. How scandalous.

Chastity swirled inside her mouth with her tongue, and a hot flush spread across her cheeks. She could still taste him. When one was desperate, one would do and propose all sorts of things. As Chastity just discovered.

"Where to?" his lordship asked.

"Drop me at the alley," she murmured.

"Shag Alley, Taylor."

That the lord's coachman knew the location of the infamous alley revealed all she needed to know. He was one of the fancy toffs seeking a cheap thrill, for there were enough of them slinking about the East End. She had heard about them and seen them. One group was called The Rakes of St. Regent's Park. Was this man one of them? She wouldn't be surprised. These nobs seemed to run about London in packs, like wild wolves out for a kill.

Chastity cringed inwardly, and then a horrid perception gripped her hard. This money would not last forever. She would no doubt be spending much of her future in that smelly, filthy lane—or somewhere similar.

Eventually, she would be forced into the streets again, perhaps permanently. The swaying of the carriage caused her stomach to roil. Choking back a sob, she clutched the bundles tighter.

No tears.

Chastity must remain resolute and stay strong, not only for herself but for her siblings. But staying strong was becoming increasingly complex, for she was weary to her bones. Beaten down by life, as the saying goes. She never understood its meaning—until now.

They did not speak, but Chastity could feel his intense stare in the dark surroundings. When the carriage rolled to a stop, she opened the door and jumped down, not waiting for the driver to assist her as if he would. Without looking back, she headed toward the dosshouse and her miserable existence.

Goodbye, Lord Ash.

ASHER PUSHED ASIDE the curtain and watched Chastity Armitage hurry past the alley and continue down the road. Pain tore through his heart, along with an undeniable fact—he couldn't let her go.

Rather a disturbing prospect.

Despite the covetousness he'd experienced when observing her at the ball long ago, emotions far beyond the physical had also gripped him. He could admit it now: Asher had been wholly besotted. His heart had swelled for the first time in his life, much like it was doing now.

Chastity disappeared; the heavy gray fog swallowed up her delicate form.

I want her.

For what, his mistress?

The option held merit, and he seriously considered it. Chastity could stay at his townhouse in Mayfair and her upkeep seen to.

No, that would not be proper. Or would it? Where did men hide away their paramours?

Asher never had one before. A long-term commitment had never appealed to him or his friends. The Rakes enjoyed the freedom of attending to numerous women at either brothels or other exclusive clubs: no emotions involved, no real intimacy beyond sex. Things were uncomplicated, just the way Asher liked it. Asher also preferred the quick tup whether he paid for it or not. Once he found his pleasure, he never gave the woman in question any further consideration.

And they never gave him any thought either.

He was the very definition of an unfeeling rake.

In truth, he could be a cold bastard. It is an ignorant man who does not know his soul—and recognize the darkness lurking within. No, he dismissed the mistress option. Asher would not make such a proposal. It did not sit well with him. The fact that he even considered it turned his bile.

But what happened to Chastity that she ended up dressed in rags?

Yes, he had come full circle to the original reason he had taken her to that horrid room above the pub. Her miserable excuse of a stepfather had told him the Armitage children were residing in Northern Scotland.

What had become of her siblings?

Asher just recalled that she had them. A younger brother and sister? Now there were even more questions. Sir Nigel had told a blatant lie. He'd been entirely convincing. Unless Chastity had run from Scotland, why return to London? Perhaps a heartbreaking tragedy befell her?

Blast it; Asher must find out the particulars of her story, which had been his original intent in the first place.

He should never have allowed her to leave the carriage.

Asher banged on the wall, and the window slid open. "Follow the young lady."

Chapter 4

THE DOOR HINGES CREAKED as Chastity stepped into the dim, cold room. There was no money for a candle or any other lighting; things had become that dire.

"Jon? Hannah?"

"Hannah is asleep," Jon whispered from the dark corner.

Her 14-year-old brother's voice hovered between a child's squeak and a man's deep tone. Already he stood taller than her but far too thin. A growing boy needed nourishment.

Chastity felt her way to the small, three-legged table. "Come, I have bread and cheese. Eat, Jon. We'll save some for Hannah."

Jon's cold fingers brushed by hers as he greedily grabbed the bread. "What about you?"

"I've eaten. I brought this for you both. And I have money."

A chilly silence filled the room. "What did you do for the money and food?"

Embarrassment and shame covered her. Even though she could not see Jon in the darkness, she felt his censure. "Nothing untoward." At least, not when one was desperate.

A knock at the door startled her.

Oh, not the landlord, not tonight.

"Don't answer it," Jon rasped, mouth full of food.

"I must. If it's Mr. Jones, I would rather pay him what we owe and be done with it."

Chastity opened the door and gasped at the sight. From the illumination of the solitary burning gaslight in the hall, she could make out the tall, broad-shouldered form of Lord Ash.

He stepped inside but did not close the door. "Do you not have any light?" he asked.

"Chastity, who is it?" Hannah cried from the bed. She started coughing, and the sound caused Chastity's heart to beat faster with worry.

"It's all right, love. Go back to sleep," she replied soothingly.

Mortified, Chastity grabbed Ash's elbow and steered him into the hall, closing the door behind her.

"Why are you here?" she whispered furiously.

"Who is in the room with you?" he demanded.

"My younger brother and sister. The food is for them. And no, I haven't any money for candles or anything else. Why do you suppose I propositioned you?"

How dare this man pursue me!

Chastity had been so caught up in desolate thoughts that she had no idea anyone had followed her. She must be more careful in the future. And she thought she had been so clever exiting the carriage at the alley. In her anxiousness to return with the food, Chastity never bothered to look behind her and see if the carriage had followed her.

Lord Ash frowned, glancing about the dirty hallway—noise from the adjoining rooms filtered through the paper-thin walls. Children cried, a man yelled obscenities, and a woman sobbed mournfully.

Welcome to life in the lower classes, my lord.

"You will not stay here another night. Gather your things and your siblings. You're coming with me," he stated in a firm voice.

What did he say? The man had lost his mind.

"I owe money for the rent—"

"I will send payment to whoever owns this blasted hovel tomorrow. In the meantime, this is no place for you, Chastity Armitage."

She gasped in horror.

Good heavens, he knows my name.

A rolling panic twisted along her spine, causing her legs to wobble. Chastity clutched his arm, and hard muscle flexed under her touch.

"You cannot tell a soul. Especially not my stepfather!"

"We will discuss that at length and at a later time. I will take you to my town house, where you will be my guests."

Surely, he spoke in jest. How would he explain bringing three ragamuffins off the streets? "Why would you do this?"

Call her suspicious, but her inner alarm started to ring incessantly. On the one hand, this offer was her wildest dream come true. To have a safe place to live, if only for a few days or weeks? On the other hand, this man was a complete stranger—of a sort, regardless of the intimacies shared.

"Do not think me benevolent," Ash replied, watching her closely.

"Of course, I understand your meaning. I suppose you shall require certain compensation for your generosity," Chastity stated. "Very well, I will be your mistress."

"I said you were to come as my guests," he murmured.

"I cannot come to your house unless I'm in your employ. And unless you need a maid or housekeeper, a mistress is the only option. You followed me here. You enjoyed what passed between us at the tavern. You want more." She spoke matter-of-factly and truthfully. There was no use beating about the bush; here was an opportunity, and she must set the terms upfront.

Chastity released his arm. Servicing him would be better than hanging about a grubby alley and being taken against the bricks by a rough-handling man who smelled of urine and sweat. She *must* secure a position—any position—for the sake of her siblings, and this was the only possibility open to her. The only option with a veneer of permanence.

How long had she tried to obtain any respectable employment? Longer than she cared to admit.

"Yes, I want more. And I do not require a maid or housekeeper," his lordship replied.

"There it is. What other option is there?"

"You could allow me to assist you, regardless."

Chastity raised her chin. "I earn my way." Apparently, she hadn't lost her stubborn streak after all. Besides, going as his guests meant they could be tossed into the streets again in a day or two. As his paid paramour, they could stay a few months at least. It would be enough time to recover from their ordeal and save a little money. And make plans for a better and hopefully brighter future.

"Well, I am not looking for a mistress, either."

"Well, those are the options," she replied firmly. Chastity must stand her ground.

She knew men of the peerage employed mistresses; she'd heard the talk. By the sheer number of women selling their wares in the streets and the noisy and raucous activity in Shag Alley alone, it seemed all of London did nothing but—what vulgar word had he used?

Fuck.

It wasn't the first time she had heard it; it would not be the last.

Chastity glanced up at his handsome face. The shadow from the yellow gaslight reflected off the sharp angles and sculpted perfection of his features. How she wished this stunning man was different from the rest. Lord Ash possessed the look of a storybook hero, yet underneath lay a rake of dubious morals. She would ensure he paid well if he decided to buy or rent her body in the short term.

"That is the only reason you would come with me? To be my mistress?" he asked, studying her closely again.

She nodded briskly.

"Very well. Then you shall be my mistress."

"I will require a salary and schooling for my brother and sister. I will *not* be separated from them, not after all this," she stated, keeping her tone resolute. Though deep down, her insides were in knots.

"Will you, indeed? How mercenary. We will work out the terms tomorrow. Even draw up a contract if you wish." He whispered in her ear, "I will have you in my bed. And I promise you will enjoy it."

His sultry breath fanned her cheeks, making them flush. Lord Ash continued to watch her intently, no doubt gauging her reaction. His features stayed neutral. Did he expect her to balk at his lewd suggestion? Withdrawal her proposal? Not with her family's survival on the line.

"You still wish to come with me, knowing your duties? You are aware of what your offer signifies?" Lord Ash asked.

In Chastity's despairing mind, she had no recourse but to make this offer. Her family's future was too uncertain. However, starvation and death seemed a sure outcome if they continued as they were. This way, as his mistress, there would be guaranteed money, a contract, and schooling for her brother and sister. Whereas any other scenario would not have any guarantees.

"Yes, I am aware. I will come with you," Chastity answered. Another horrible thought entered her swirling and confused thoughts. "How do I know you will not take me somewhere, violate me, and then toss me to the cobbles? Or worse, do murder?"

He trailed two fingers across her cheek, and his touch scorched her skin. "If I had a violation in mind, I would have done so at the inn. It's either me or this deplorable subsistence. It doesn't leave you with much choice. I can see why you made the offer."

After barely surviving calamitous circumstances for nearly three years, how could she live with herself if she condemned her siblings to continue in such a dreadful existence?

None of them were thriving.

They were emaciated, pale, and—she glanced at the dirt under her broken nails—filthy. She tried to keep them and the room clean, but it was a battle lost. Soap was too expensive to purchase when food and firewood were needed more.

Hannah had turned sickly the past several months and couldn't work for long periods. Even now, she experiences constant congestion in her chest. One whiff of illness could be fatal. Her brother had taken to thievery in their more dreadful moments, and Chastity feared his arrest. Jon needed education and guidance. Darkness resided in his gaze, and she remained afraid to ask about it.

And herself?

What did it matter?

Ruined.

Not that society would have given her much of a chance. She came from a middle-class home where they were all content enough. At the time, Chastity understood that she would never move about in the upper echelons of society. What man of the peerage, or one connected to it, would consider a solicitor's daughter for a possible marriage? And she hardly cared, for she had been satisfied enough with her station.

Before her father died, he had claimed that a young man studying to be a doctor had wanted to make her acquaintance. The introduction never came to pass. Chastity mourned her former life when she allowed herself to mire in self-pity.

What she would give to be there again. But her safe and content life had been a sham.

When her father died, leaving them penniless, they were nearly tossed into the street. How ironic, for she and her siblings wound up there anyway. Little wonder that her mother accepted the first offer of marriage that came her way. They had spent four years with Nigel Barrington, a cold, distant man who hid his depraved nature under a solicitous façade.

As Chastity grew older, she noticed the pained grimace on her mother's face on certain mornings. God knows what the man had done to her in the privacy of their bedroom.

If her mother could make the ultimate sacrifice for her children, she could do no less for her brother and sister.

The unvarnished truth?

She would be a prostitute with one exclusive client.

Weighing her options, Chastity acknowledged becoming a mistress beat being a three-penny-upright in a dark alley.

Yes, she was right to make the offer.

Ash gripped her chin, tilting her face upward to look at him. So handsome. Lord Ash's touch was electric.

But what dissolute wickedness lurked beneath his polite and polished veneer? It looked as if she would soon find out.

"This is your final decision?" he questioned flatly.

There was only one answer she could give.

"Yes. This is my final decision."

What the future would bring, Chastity did not even want to consider. It was only the present she had to be concerned with.

Food. Warmth. Money.

The safety of her brother and sister.

Nothing else mattered.

Nothing.

Chapter 5

THIRTY MINUTES LATER, Asher arrived at his residence with his guests in tow. Grimes, his venerated butler, looked aghast at the state of the Armitage family but quickly shuttered his gaze to reflect his usual unruffled and professional bearing.

"Fetch Mrs. Brindle, Grimes. See that Miss Hannah and Master Jon are properly bathed and fed. Prepare the attic rooms for them. Burn the rags they're wearing, and find something clean and appropriate for sleeping."

He clutched Chastity's arm. "Miss Armitage and I have much to discuss. We will be in the study and not to be disturbed."

"Of course, my lord. I will see it done. Shall I bring tea?"

"Yes. A little food would not go amiss. Whatever is available in the larder. Feed the children as well. I do not want a fuss. I don't want any discussion as to the identity of my guests—or the fact that I have any guests at all."

Grimes gave a quick nod and a bow. The butler would see that there would be no gossiping outside the town house walls. Asher's staff was loyal. He paid them well and treated them respectfully, partly to ensure their steadfastness.

As he passed the butler his hat and cloak, he leaned in and whispered, "I will reveal more details later, Grimes. I've rescued them from a horrendous situation. I'm acquainted with the young lady, and she and her family do not deserve such a fate."

"We will see them well looked after, my lord," Grimes replied firmly.

"Good man."

Asher steered Chastity toward the study. Motioning to the sofa, he bade her sit. She removed her thread-bare bonnet and laid it next to her.

The Armitages brought little with them. The siblings each clutched a pathetic bundle to their chests. Asher wagered that the belongings should be burned.

The clock on the mantel chimed eleven. Asher should allow her to bathe and get some sleep but damn it; there would be no slumber for him until he knew more of Chastity's situation. Might as well put it out there.

"Why would Barrington say you all left London to live with distant relatives in Scotland?" he asked.

Genuine surprise flickered across Chastity's weary features. "Is that what the wretched man said? My God." She rubbed her hands in obvious irritation. "How is it you know my name? And how do you know my stepfather?"

Asher sat opposite. Why prevaricate? Might as well tell the truth. "I saw you at Durham's ball about three years ago. You made quite an impression on me. Before I could obtain an introduction, you had departed the gathering. I eventually found out who you were, and I badgered my father until he consented to escort me to your home."

He removed his cloak and tossed it on the nearby chair. "Having my baron father there with me would make a better impression. Or so I believed at the time. Regardless, when we arrived on your doorstep three weeks after the ball, Barrington informed us that you had departed for Scotland, never to return."

Asher paused. "You ran away, didn't you? Why? Surely there was someone you could have gone to instead of trying to make your way on the streets."

Red rage glowed in her weary eyes. "If there were anyone we could have turned to, we would have asked for assistance. We have no relatives, at least none that I knew. My father died penniless and in debt. We learned just how terrible the state of affairs was after he passed. Bad investments, we were told. My mother and I had no idea our situation was so perilous."

Chastity rubbed her forehead, then continued, "His few friends and colleagues turned from our family long ago. When my mother married Barrington shortly after my father's death—a marriage she had to make, or we would have been ruined—Barrington's friends became hers. Not that he had that many friends. We were fleeing from *him*. We couldn't go to any of Sir Nigel's acquaintances. There was no one, I tell you. No one." Her voice was emphatic.

Tears threatened, and Asher could see her struggle to remain in control. A sick feeling settled deep inside him.

"What did this man do to you all?"

Chastity gulped. "I will tell you that Barrington is depraved. Draw your conclusions from that. When my mother passed, he made it plain what he wished. He had special plans for us all, especially for Jon. I could *not* allow it. The situation became so fraught with danger that I started sleeping in Jon's room. One night, Sir Nigel crept in, and I knocked him senseless. We fled without looking back."

Chastity's fierceness in protecting her siblings was admirable. Then hot fury replaced Asher's esteem. Damn Barrington for taking advantage of three impoverished orphans. There was more to this story, which churned his guts to guess at what.

Grimes entered carrying a tea tray with assorted sandwiches and fresh fruit and placed it on the table between them.

"We can look after ourselves, Grimes. Have the rooms adjoining mine made up, and a hot bath poured for Miss Chastity. Then have one of the maids come and fetch her in thirty minutes."

Placing Chastity in the rooms next to his? It said plenty about what her status would be. Chastity frowned briefly but said nothing.

"As you wish, my lord," Grimes replied. The butler closed the door behind him.

A look of ravenous hunger spread across Chastity's face.

Good God, to be that famished. May he never know the feeling.

"Will you pour? Are you able?" he asked.

She flashed him a scathing look. "I haven't forgotten parlor manners."

Tired, drained, and beaten down by circumstance, she still showed courage and determination. The truth of it? Asher genuinely wished to assist her and her siblings. Her being his mistress had not entered his mind, not seriously. Only that brief, fleeting moment, then he immediately dismissed the terrible idea. But since she suggested it first and made it a condition, he would play along if it meant that she would stay.

"Then, by all means, pour. Now, to continue about Barrington. How old are you? Does he have guardianship over you all?"

Chastity squirmed in her seat. "I will be twenty-four in two months. Sir Nigel has no claim on me, not any longer, but he is the legal guardian of Hannah and Jon."

"You know this for a fact? Were you shown legal papers?"

"Well, no. Why do you suppose I fled with my siblings? To protect them. I couldn't leave them in his care. But after my mother passed, Sir Nigel's solicitor told me the courts sanctioned a written agreement. Not after he had made it plain what he wanted."

This situation could be a legal and societal muddle. Barrington could petition the court to return the Armitages to him, at least the two younger ones. Asher knew nothing of guardianship or adoption, only that there were no permanent laws protecting children. It is why orphans roamed the streets without any care from the state. It was shameful.

But a guardianship? The court would consider the younger children Barrington's possessions legally obtained and would no doubt rule them returned to his supervision as if they were chattel. Which they were, legally speaking. Or so Asher surmised.

"We will speak more of Barrington later. But for now, we will discuss our arrangement. You will be in the rooms next to mine. There is an adjourning door. If you are to be my mistress as you say, know that I'll be visiting you quite often as I'm of an amorous nature. Will you become all missish about coupling with me with your brother and sister under the same roof?"

Her hand shook as she poured the tea, but she didn't reply.

Perhaps he was playing the role too well. But he had to make Chastity believe this agreement was going forward until he figured out how to assist her and her siblings in the long term.

Asher reached for the cup and saucer and stroked her fingers. Just that slight contact heated his blood to the boiling point.

"Shall we agree on a term length for this affair?" He sat back and took a sip, keeping his voice formal.

This entire "mistress" conversation was surreal. But if it kept her here under his roof and his protection, as it were, he would go along with the ruse.

"I will agree to whatever terms you set," Chastity replied quietly and respectfully.

Asher did not care for this subdued Chastity. He preferred it when her chin was raised in stubborn defiance, her eyes flashing with heated emotion. The thought of unleashing all that passion in bed again stirred his arousal to life.

Perhaps having her here was not judicious after all.

"For God's sake, Chastity. Don't stand on ceremony, eat. When was the last time you ate fresh grapes?"

Without hesitation, she filled her plate. It warmed Asher to see her partake of nourishment, but he remained outwardly devoid of emotion.

"Let us say—one year. With an option to renew," Asher said.

Good God, it sounded as if he negotiated rent on a dwelling. He had no intention of keeping her here for a year.

Asher understood from some of his acquaintances that one year was the standard contract.

"I will employ a governess for Jon and Hannah since you wish them to continue their education. I will feed and clothe them as I will you. Also, I will provide an allowance and pin money to spend or save as you please. Are you with me so far? Do you agree?"

"That is generous. I agree."

"At the end of the one year, you will earn three hundred pounds," Asher continued. "Any clothes or gifts I deem fit to bestow on you are yours to keep. We will discuss new terms if you wish to remain my mistress after one year. Is that satisfactory?"

Chastity ate with some haste but daintily, proving that she possessed good manners. She reached for more fruit and another sandwich. "And if you should tire of me before the year ends, what then, my lord?"

As if that would happen.

If Chastity knew how ferociously he desired her, how fiercely his blood raged, she would run screaming from the room.

How tempting to give in to his desire. Carry Chastity to his room, tear those rags from her, and take possession. Thrust into her wet heat, but give her pleasure in return, until she writhed in his arms, moaning—hell, what had she asked him?

Right. The contract.

"Then the contract is broken, and I will pay you the three hundred pounds regardless," he said. "And I said you are to call me Ash."

She frowned into her cup. "I cannot understand why you agreed to this."

Did she have any idea at all of how beautiful she was, inside and out?

He wished to see her hale and hearty again. Granted, she stood a pale comparison to the young lady he'd observed at the ball, but a few weeks of good eating would fill those lush curves to their previous state. It would put color back in her pale cheeks as well.

Most of all, he wanted to banish the weariness that oozed from her every pore.

Society dictated that he keep this arrangement professional and detached. Isn't that how rich men acted with mistresses? They were on retainer to perform a service, nothing more, which is why he had mentioned the contract. And why he agreed to her proposal in order to remove her from those horrid, dank rooms.

It would be wise to keep his distance in more ways than one, at least as far as emotions were concerned—for the time being.

They had parts to play—of a lord and his employee. No emotion, no small talk, no companionship needed. What a cold prospect, indeed.

Asher should literally keep his distance for a few days at least until he gains control of his wayward feelings. This entire situation played havoc on his inner reserve.

"Tomorrow morning, I will move temporarily to my club. It's wise that I keep separate lodgings until you're settled and somewhat recovered from your ordeal. Then we will discuss other permanent accommodations for the future. You and your brother and sister cannot remain here long-term. And you do not need to know why I want you. Do you agree to the terms? I will have the contract drawn up tomorrow."

Chastity placed her cup and saucer on the tray. Lifting her head, she met his gaze. No emotion showed on her face.

"I agree. And I assure you I will not become missish over this pact. My brother and sister will be told of the circumstances and accept the situation. I ask one thing of you in return. I do not want my stepfather to know we are here."

Asher had several more questions, but they could wait. "I will not tell him; you have my word. I have no contact with the man."

The maid entered and escorted Chastity to her room.

Asher slumped in his chair and nibbled absently on a cucumber and cheese sandwich. He had a distinct feeling that he'd taken on far more than intended.

Damn his desire.

Because deep down, he knew. His acceptance of Chastity's offer was not entirely steeped in giving aid to those less fortunate, though that factored into his agreement.

He wanted *her*.

And he wanted Chastity to want him.

Not as an employee or as a hired mistress. But as herself. How can that be achieved? One step at a time.

Then he could plan what to do next. First, get Chastity settled in and adequately fed. Her brother and sister, too. Asher could not allow them to stay another night in those horrible, lonely rooms.

He lived in a protective bubble; he knew that. Asher had never wanted for anything in his entire life. Even though many in the peerage had seen their fortunes reduced over the years, the Wenlock baronetcy was in robust shape. Asher would hazard to guess that his fortune outweighed all the other rakes in his group combined.

But seeing how people lived, crammed into tiny dark rooms in rundown flats, had shaken him. It pulled him out of his elitist bubble and forced him to see what, for years, he patently ignored.

Instead of living dissolute lives and whining about boredom, he and The Rakes of St. Regent's Park could turn their attention to more worthwhile pursuits. Like assisting their fellowman. What would be the lads' reactions when he brought up that topic at their next meeting?

As for Chastity, perhaps he could secure her a respectable position outside the city limits. Christian might know of a situation or one of his other friends.

In the meantime, keep his distance.

In more ways than one.

Or his heart could be lost.

Chapter 6

CHASTITY SOAKED IN the lilac-scented water, using the time alone to gain a modicum of peace. It is the first such peace Chastity had enjoyed since before her father passed away.

Jon and Hannah had already retired to adjoining rooms in the attic. The maid, Anna, had stated that the children's sleeping chambers were clean and well-appointed. The servants had been kind, they did not look down their noses at Chastity, and for that, she was grateful. It made this transition a little easier to bear.

Chastity sighed and glanced about the room. Lord Ash possessed a modern bathing room with water from pipes attached to a gas heater. Chastity had never seen the like. What did the rest of the town house look like? Including the attic, there were four stories to the place, with multiple rooms. All richly decorated, she imagined.

Barrington entered her thoughts, causing her to frown. While living with him, her family was not what London society would consider wealthy. At least during those four years, they had been given clothes, food, and a roof over their head.

But at what price to their mother?

Chastity was ashamed to admit she had not given her poor mother much thought over the past years except in anger and disbelief. How could she marry another man so soon after Papa's death? It was shocking when three weeks after her father died, they found themselves whisked off to Sir Nigel's with the sudden news of the marriage.

They had no time to mourn the loss of their father, let alone try and understand what was happening. On top of that, how could her mother leave them in the care of her revolting husband?

Granted, there was no one else to turn to. What option did Chastity's mother have? Now that she reflected on it—none. Her mother had no choice *but* to marry.

A woman alone had no options.

Chastity understood what that entailed more than anyone. Sighing, she twirled her fingers in the fragrant water.

Before her mother died, she mentioned that Barrington had promised to see Chastity wed and settled. Since becoming Sir Nigel, the knighthood had opened doors previously closed to her middle-class background. Not all entries in the upper classes, for a knight was not part of the peerage, but at least would afford introduction to men of means.

Her mother had informed her: "You will attend balls and entertainments, introduced to men of influence and wealth, perhaps even men of the peerage. You're beautiful, my dear; surely there is a decent man who would marry you regardless of your lack of standing and dowry. Sir Nigel gave me his word. Marry well, and look after your brother and sister. That must be the plan going forward."

How could her mother know that she would die unexpectedly before the settlement of Chastity's future? That left them in Sir Nigel's care.

Of all people.

Or perhaps her mother was sick for some time and began to make plans for her children. What did it matter? The promised opportunities no longer existed. They were gone in a puff of smoke and empty pledges.

At first, Sir Nigel had kept his word as she attended two balls shortly before her mother's death. At those events, she met important and titled young men. A couple of them even showed interest.

Lord Ash saw her at one of those balls and had later sought her out? It all came too late.

Frustrated, she pounded the water with her clenched fist, the soapsuds splashing on her chest. Chastity had not indulged in these self-pitying thoughts for a long time. Why now? There would be no marriage in her future as she was well and truly ruined.

Why not embrace the next best option?

Being under the protection of an affluent baron would see them all well looked after, at least temporarily. Yes, the maid had told her his full name and title.

Lord Asher Colborne, Baron Wenlock.

She liked the name. It fit him.

Anna confided that the baronetcy dates back to the medieval era: an ancient and prosperous seat and a well-respected name known within high society and royalty circles. Anna also called him a "good master" like his father before him, who treated his servants with kindness and generosity.

He had undoubtedly acted every inch the lord when she first encountered him, except when he became flustered after her oral ministrations. She winced at thinking such a naughty thought. Lord Ash must have liked it since he sought her out and brought her here. Perhaps she would be spending much time on her knees.

Oh, heavens. A one-year contract?

Surely the negotiated situation wouldn't last that long. A handsome man of the peerage has many distractions. She would be one—for a time. Then what would happen?

Her mind raced, her thoughts pinging in all directions forming scenarios and possible outcomes. The main goal here was to save every shilling. If Chastity earned hundreds of pounds, the future for her and her siblings would be brighter. It would open many doors of opportunities.

It could be accomplished. She would throw herself into her work and show as much enthusiasm as possible. Initiate the encounters to keep his lordship's interest. The sooner they consummated the agreement, the better. It would solidify her standing and give her a sense of permanency, if only in the short term. Feeling secure in this strange scenario would assist in their recovery, even if it was temporary.

Chastity's thoughts drifted to her brother. Jon could apprentice in some respectable trade. How unfortunate she could not sew worth a farthing. Dressmakers would not hire her, although she'd tried many times to obtain employment at various shops. Chastity also tried steam laundries and street stalls selling vegetables or fish. Nothing ever panned out for steady work. It was as if the fates were against her at every turn.

Not anymore.

Should she insist that Lord Ash find her a decent position somewhere after he had tired of her? Yes, a definite addendum to the contract. Employment as a companion or in a high-end retail shop. Something to bring in a steady and reliable income. Or were companions a thing of the past? Whatever decent employment could be achieved.

Another urgent topic drifted into her mind: children.

There were ways to prevent it. Chastity heard prossies talking about such possibilities in the alley. The last thing Chastity wanted was to be with child. Then again, she would be set for life, wouldn't she? Didn't men generally look after their illegitimate offspring?

No, not at all.

She knew of more than a few ladies working the streets who were by-blows of various members of the aristocracy. Chastity didn't like that term, but it is what the women referred to themselves as.

No one looked after them.

No one cared.

Another addition to the document: the prevention of pregnancy.

Chastity became so lost in thought that she did not hear the door open.

"Enjoying your bath?"

The deep, masculine tone shocked her back to reality. She lowered herself in the tub until the waterline and lingering suds hid her breasts.

How silly. I'm to be Lord Ash's mistress.

"Yes, thank you," she responded.

Ash stood at the foot of the tub with arms akimbo. He looked disheveled and piratical, wearing black trousers and a white shirt open to the waistband. An expanse of his powerfully-built chest showed to advantage, and Chastity bit her lip to stifle a soft moan at the delicious sight.

"I thought you were taking separate lodgings and keeping your distance?" Chastity exclaimed. Best to change the subject and keep her mind off his enticing presence.

"Tomorrow. And as for keeping my distance? It appears that I cannot stay away. I informed Anna that I would see to you."

He pulled over a stool and sat next to her. After rolling up his sleeves, Ash rubbed the cloth with soap. "Sit forward. I will wash your back."

He sat with his legs spread and the material molded to him. His forearms were muscular and dusted lightly with black hair. While his voice was soft, it also held a husky cadence. Such intoxicating masculinity. What did it matter if Ash saw her naked?

Grasping the sides of the clawfoot tub, she leaned forward. Slowly, Ash swirled the cloth about her back in a seductive manner.

"I-I thought of a couple of items to add to the contract," she ventured.

"Did you, indeed?"

His touch was magic. Ash moved his cloth-covered hand lower to the top of her buttocks, stroking with such concentration, such—skill.

"I will require that my brother learns a respectable trade or becomes an apprentice in one. He must have a chance at life. Some alternate employment should be investigated for me as well. Also, I want to prevent children."

The words tumbled out of her so fast that she wondered if Ash even understood what she said.

He gently pushed her upright and swirled the cloth across her breasts. "You are far too thin. We will remedy that."

Chastity shuddered with desire at his ministrations.

"You do not need to fear me. While I enjoy a quick rut, I can be a considerate and thorough lover when I put my mind to it," he said. "Take satisfaction and pleasure in the fact that you will bring me to my knees. I will do for you what you did for me."

Ash had interpreted her trembling as fear when it was from desire. She would not tell him any different.

Ash spread her legs, and the fabric stroked between them. "I will lick and taste you here until you beg me for release." The cloth made a quick motion to arrive at her breasts again. Her nipples hardened into painful peaks. "You're so responsive. I will lick and suck you here until you are wet and plead for me to take you," he continued in a low voice.

"I will never beg."

Deliberately, he continued to stroke her nipples. "Yes. You will. And I believe you will make a beggar of me. We will enjoy ourselves, Chastity. There is much more to sex than being taken against a wall—though the position has merit."

She could not take much more of this. Already a deluge of sensations tore through her at his nearness as he explored her with such capable thoroughness.

Keep your head, Chastity, think.

"You did not answer my question. What of children?" she asked.

"There will be none. I will use French letters. We will not make a child; I will see to it."

Ash dipped the cloth in the water and continued his methodical exploration across her chest and between her legs. They parted of their own accord to allow him access.

"I am to trust you, then?"

"Yes. Leave it with me. I will make inquiries for your brother as well. He should have a trade or occupation. And for yourself, if you like."

Chastity exhaled in relief. Ash's face held such an intense concentration on his task. As far as the trust that had to be earned. She would make sure he used protection.

"What are French letters?" she asked.

A brief bark of laughter left his throat. "My God, you are innocent. They are also called sheaths. I wear it on my shaft, and my seed collects so it will not take root in you."

"I would prefer if you used the sheaths in all our interactions," she murmured.

"I said I would." His half-lidded, sensual stare seared her. "Did you feel that? Every nerve ending has sparked to life. You, my dear, are aroused."

He dropped the cloth in the water and stood, his prominent erection at her eye level.

"So are you, Baron Wenlock."

What possessed her to say that in such a sultry manner? This strange relationship appeared to be moving forward of its own accord. The room, already warm and humid from the bath, shot a couple of degrees higher.

"Perhaps we should dispense with contracts and proprieties and rut each other right now," he growled seductively.

Lord Ash affected her. Her insides dipped and rolled excitedly at the prospect. It was not very prudent, but she couldn't help it. She could not think of anything to say in response.

"Nevertheless, I'm not a complete beast. You need your rest. Goodnight, Chastity." He gave her a curt bow and strode from the room.

The door closed, and none too softly. Chastity trembled with unfulfilled desire. Yes, she would make the first initiation into this salacious contract. Best to get it out of the way and shore up this arrangement. Having relations with Lord Ash might also rid her of this annoying attraction that continued to pop up whenever he was near.

Chastity should not and could not act on it.

Regardless, she had the distinct feeling she had just stepped into a lion's den.

Chapter 7

"WAKE UP, CHASTITY!"

Groaning, she sat upright as her vision came into focus. It took a moment to realize where she was. Exhaustion had overcome her last night, and because of it, she hadn't had a chance to inspect the room.

It consisted of sturdy oak furnishings, and the four-poster bed was large and comfortable. The color scheme showed a feminine touch with rosebud wallpaper and creamy fleur-de-lis contrasts. On the mantel sat a lovely clock with white and gold accents. Good heavens, it was half past ten. She had slept nearly around the clock.

Jon and Hannah stood by her bed wearing oversized nightshirts.

"We've had our breakfast. A maid brought it to our rooms, can you imagine?" Hannah chattered, livelier than Chastity had seen the 11-year-old girl for a long time. "Porridge, toast, fresh fruit, pastries, and I ate it all, and so did Jon!"

Chastity smiled warmly at her sister's unbridled enthusiasm. Seeing this innocent reaction to a decent breakfast made her decision easier. Jon, however, remained sullen and silent. He had no doubt guessed why they resided at a wealthy lord's town house.

"We should take care not to overeat at first. We're not used to large portions and don't want to make ourselves sick."

Hannah nodded in agreement.

"I have something to tell you both. I am in Baron Wenlock's employ. There will be a one-year contract with a salary and incentives, including a governess for you both and eventually an apprenticeship for you, Jon."

Her brother curled his lip in disgust.

Confusion crossed Hannah's features. "Are you to be his housekeeper?" she questioned.

"No, my dear. I'm to be—" How mortifying. How to explain to a guileless girl?

"His whore," Jon spat. "I heard your conversation with him in the hallway last night. Every blasted word."

Hannah gasped. They knew the word well enough and had heard it shouted many times in the hallways at the dosshouse.

Anger tore through Chastity's veins. She scrambled from the bed, clutched her brother's arm, and shook him firmly. "Would you prefer that we stay in that miserable room without money for food, heat, or light? Starving to death? Or would you prefer the workhouse; and never see each other again? I'm doing this so we will have a future, especially you, Jon! I will not have you disrespect me—or Baron Wenlock. This is a perfectly acceptable arrangement in the higher rank of society, and you know it."

She grasped his chin and made him look at her. "Or would you rather we return to Sir Nigel, where he would press his immoral advances on you and Hannah?" It was horrible to say, but she must make her brother understand her reasoning and why she made this difficult decision.

Tears welled in Jon's blue eyes. "It's my fault we had to leave! If only I did what he wanted," he sobbed.

What fresh horror was this?

Jon wiped his eyes on the sleeve of his nightshirt. "Do *not* ask me."

Her heart ached for them all. No wonder Jon's face appeared haunted at times. They had put off this discussion long enough. Chastity loathed mentioning this in front of their younger sister, but it was about time she understood the circumstances of their plight.

"Did he hurt you?" she asked, her voice shaking.

"I said don't ask me." Jon's voice was gruff, then he sniffled.

"Did. He. Hurt. You? Yes or no." Chastity fought to keep her voice even. Her heart ached at the prospect of either of her siblings being harmed in any way. "You understand what I am asking you?"

"Yes, I understand. The answer is no. And I don't want to talk about it," Jon hissed through clenched teeth.

The relief that flooded Chastity at hearing Jon had not been violated—at least physically—was palatable. But the damage had been done, nonetheless. Giving her brother a thorough look, Chastity decided her brother told the truth—or part of it. Or did he lie out of shame?

"Very well, Jon. But you must accept the current circumstances and take advantage of the opportunities. There will be clean clothes, food, a warm fire, education, good health, and the possibility of a decent occupation and a solid future. To give you both all this and more, I would sacrifice anything. Do—*anything*. Do you comprehend what I am saying?"

Jon nodded; his lower lip trembled. He fought back the tears. So was Chastity.

Hannah's eyes were as round as saucers. Did her younger sister even know what they were talking about? Judging by her shocked expression, Hannah had an inkling.

Chastity lamented this more than anything—the loss of innocence—for all of them. Especially Jon and Hannah. Their childhood had been ripped from them. Many nights, they shivered in their cold hovel; she wondered if keeping them all together was selfish on her part.

Perhaps. In fact, yes. It had been.

It could be argued that the workhouse or the orphanage would be a different torment. One frantic afternoon months ago, Chastity stopped by a workhouse and was appalled at the conditions. An orphanage wouldn't have been much better. But then, her siblings might have been adopted by decent people and given a home. Or not. In either situation, they would have been separated, probably never to see each other again.

Too late for regrets.

Chastity had to think of the present. And the family's collective survival.

"Baron Wenlock is not a cruel man from what I perceive. He will not treat me ill. Promise me you will grant his lordship the respect that he deserves."

Jon nodded again, then threw his arms around her neck. He was still a little lad in many ways. Struggling to keep the emotions at bay, she hugged him in return. Hannah joined their embrace.

Deep down, she surmised that the baron would not be cruel, but who knew?

For her brother and sister, she would forfeit *everything*.

THE NEXT DAY PASSED in a blur. Asher's solicitor arrived in the afternoon, and Chastity finalized and signed the contract. He never had his residence see such activity.

My God, I am actually going through with this.

Asher had brought up the subject of a contract to show her he was serious about the mistress proposal. It was a way to keep her here until he found them a better situation. He never believed they would draw up an agreement. This ruse, however well-meaning, was starting to take on a life of its own. And Asher was in danger of losing control of the narrative.

The dressmakers arrived next, taking measurements of the Armitages and procuring sturdy, clean, secondhand clothing until the new garments were ready. He had paid a king's ransom to hurry along with the order, though the cost hardly mattered.

Alone in his rooms later that night, Asher's thoughts slid to his late father, an honorable man who had stayed faithful to his dead wife even five years after her passing. His father had never taken a mistress, as far as Asher knew. His father was in the minority of those in the peerage.

Wonder what he would think of this arrangement?

The late baron had never admonished Asher on his wild and wicked ways, as Asher did not indulge excessively or allow it to interfere with his duties. Although his father tsked when he joined The Rakes of St. Regent's Park, he never called attention to it incessantly. Asher stated he had joined more for the social aspect than any true debauchery; he explained that most of the men in the group were his childhood friends. His father sighed, nodded, and headed to his study.

Since becoming Baron Wenlock, Asher has followed in his late father's footsteps and has taken his responsibilities seriously. He ran his father's vast holdings with a deft and frugal hand—along with the steward and the household staff, of course—keeping his extracurricular activities far removed from the baronetcy.

Now he would have new responsibilities: Chastity and her family.

Quite an undertaking.

And so much for his declaration of staying away. Last night, as soon as he had found out she was taking a bath, he impulsively entered the room. He had acted every inch the superior lord. By God, seeing her lounging in a tub full of bubbles had nearly brought him to his knees.

Pacing about the room, Asher rubbed his hands in irritation. His thoughts returned to the squalid room above the inn. His reaction to her sucking him had turned him into a puddle of submissive desire.

Not a reaction he was entirely accustomed to.

The kiss affected him more, if that were possible, flustering him to such an extent that he had escaped before revealing more of his feelings than he wished to. Hence his swift exit and escorting Chastity to the alley. Once the thick fog swallowed her, he realized he did not want her to go. Against all logic, he had followed her to her pathetic lodgings. Quite the impulsive behavior on all fronts, which proved his emotions were a complete wreck.

The die is cast.

Asher had a sinking feeling when they finally consummated their arrangement—if they did—it would change everything. He'd kept emotion and sentiment out of his past assignations. Stay detached, take his pleasure, and move on.

He must ensure it transpired here. The young woman was in his employ, if temporarily.

Why was guilt picking at his soul if this arrangement was perfectly acceptable and commonly done? Was he taking advantage of a desperate young woman? Even though he had only agreed to her suggestion to be his mistress to assist her? And why was he overthinking this?

Legally, she was his mistress.

They could move forward with the physical aspect. Chastity had acted sensually last night while bathing.

Or was it wishful thinking on his part?

The clock on the mantel read ten o'clock. As Asher paced about his room like a caged lion, he pulled the sash on his dressing gown tighter. He wore nothing underneath but a pair of trousers. Already he was stiff and aching as he'd been on and off since her arrival.

Last night in the bath, washing her had aroused him to such an extent that he gave himself release twice during the night. The imperious manner in which he'd exited was false at its core.

The sole reason is that he had to depart before making a fool of himself. Asher would have dropped to his knees and begged her to suck him again, kiss him and hold him in her embrace—to make love to him without the enticement of coin, contract, and clauses.

Control rapidly slipped away the more he was in her presence, a prospect he thought he would never find himself in with any woman.

He would be her abject and worshipful—what, exactly?

Isn't that what he'd desired, a woman who would enslave him heart and soul and be willing to allow the same with her? He yearned for an intelligent, passionate woman who would stand up to him and share his life, dreams, and darkest desires.

Where had he hoped to find this paragon of female passion if his latest conquests consisted of older widows and younger prossies?

Yet, he believed that Chastity could be everything he gave up hope of ever finding.

In the meantime, he must remain emotionally disengaged until he knows what passions are at play. Asher took a deep breath and then exhaled. It would not be wise to reveal the countless confusing feelings inside him. Best they talk and try to navigate this emotional minefield without revealing his deepest worries and desires.

He knocked twice on the connecting door and entered the room.

Chastity sat on the edge of the bed, her glorious crown of golden-brown hair tumbling past her shoulders. She wore a prim and simple nightgown, probably borrowed from one of the maids.

The roar of desire that tore through him shocked him to his bare feet. A vision of him shredding the cotton shift from her body made his blood fire and blaze in his veins. So much for navigating that emotional minefield. Despite the fire raging within him, Asher kept his face devoid of feeling. At least, he hoped.

Chastity faced him and managed to look indifferent. Or was she masking deeper emotions as well?

"You're still here? I thought you were staying at your club temporarily," she stated, her voice even.

"I've been busy. If you like, I can go tomorrow."

"That is up to you. Your comings and goings are none of my business. Shall we get on with it and consummate this agreement?"

Asher blinked rapidly. "What?"

He had come in here to talk and nothing else. He was going to mention that they should postpone the physical aspect of their arrangement to give them both a reprieve. And give him time to take control of his wayward emotions and plan how to assist with Chastity and her family's future.

But before he could broach the subject, Chastity stood, swiftly pulled the nightgown over her head, and tossed it aside.

All thoughts of conversation left his mind. As well as all common sense. Just as before in the room at the pub.

Last night Asher had admired her naked form, which was visible through the bath bubbles, but standing before him, completely exposed, he took his time and savored the view. Such beautiful silky skin to admire and worship. Chastity's breasts were not small, but neither overlarge. She was gorgeous.

Asher hardened further. And with that, the last of his restrained control fled.

Loosening the sash, he let the dressing gown slither to the floor. Chastity's eyes widened, and her gaze grew heated.

Asher kept himself in shape with various sporting activities such as riding, boxing, and fencing. He indulged in sporadic physical labor at Wenlock Manor to stay active and fit. Many women had admired his form in the past, but seeing her appreciation made his heart swell with masculine satisfaction.

She lay crosswise on the bed, her legs dangling over the side. Moving her to the edge, Asher spread her thighs and stroked her. Wetness coated his fingers. Chastity responded with a slight moan and a slow roll of her hips.

The blood that raged through his veins thrummed and pounded in his head. Asher couldn't think straight, only feel. His mind swirled, his rational thought lost in a sensual fog.

He unfastened the buttons on his trousers. He wanted this. He wanted *her*.

"Wait," she whispered. "The French letter?"

Of course, he made a promise, and he always used them. He dashed to his room and retrieved an envelope from his bedside table. Asher returned to her side and then slipped on the condom. Perhaps he should heighten her arousal more, but his selfish needs took precedence. As always. One of his many flaws.

Looping his arms under her knees, he spread her wide and plunged in. Chastity gasped, so he stilled for a moment giving her time to adjust to him. Her feminine core clutched him in a decidedly possessive and intimate manner.

"I-I-I need—"

God, how pathetic he sounded. To hell with talking. He was lost in a fog; he couldn't even form rational thoughts, let alone speak them aloud. The less said, the better.

The thrusts were deep and fast, the bedsprings squeaking with his effort. Chastity lifted her hips to meet his fierce plunges. However, she did not touch him. She just lay open, exposed, letting him take what he needed.

But she was hardly unaffected. Soft, husky moans escaped her luscious lips, which caused Asher to pump her with wild abandon. His head swam from the intense passion possessing him.

Asher reached for that unknown place of utter bliss. A place he had never been before, but for once, it lay within his grasp. A multitude of swirling colors swam in his vision. With one final thrust, he came, hard and very loud. Maybe Asher yelled her name, but he could not be sure. He backed away and almost stumbled as his legs were like jelly.

Chastity leaned on her elbows and stared at him in puzzlement, her legs still wide.

The realization hit him that he had not seen to her pleasure at all. Instead, Asher had dismissed it and saw to it that he was satisfied.

He was an animal—an unfeeling, arrogant arse.

This is not how he wanted their first time together to be. Hell, he didn't even come into the room for this. But he allowed himself to be carried away. Once again. Asher had bungled this beyond all hope. Angry and embarrassed, Asher reached for his dressing gown and stomped from the room, slamming the door behind him.

Chapter 8

CHASTITY BLINKED, AND hot tears of frustration gathered at the corner of her eyes.

That was it? Was she that terrible?

Was her performance so inadequate that he stormed from the room? She stared at the closed connecting door in disbelief. Would this be the extent of their couplings?

The feeling of Ash filling and stretching her was almost too heavenly to bear. Yet during the brief act, he hadn't looked at her. Nor had he touched or kissed her.

But isn't that what she'd observed in the alley? Men taking their selfish pleasure? Why would his lordship be any different?

She thought—or hoped—he would be dissimilar. The kiss he had given her at the inn, passionate and powerful with such emotion behind it, had her clinging to the absurd notion that Ash cared.

Indeed, she had not imagined it.

But what did she know of deeper emotions between a man and a woman? Wiping her eyes, she reached for the nightgown, slipping it over her head. Chastity dipped the cloth in the basin and cleaned up. Since he'd worn the sheath, the only moisture between her legs belonged to her.

She shuddered as the wet fabric made contact with her sensitive area. The selfish man had left her in an aroused state. Tossing the cloth aside, she marched toward the connecting door. Leaning in, Chastity could not hear anything. After turning the handle, she slipped inside.

By the window stood the silhouette of a shirtless Ash; moonlight cast him in a splendid illumination. He leaned on a side table; his hand spread on the surface to anchor him while his other hand was clasping his—good heavens.

She glided toward him, fascinated at what he was doing.

A ragged groan escaped him as his gaze met hers. "Go back to your room," he growled as he pumped his shaft.

Chastity could plainly see the anguish on his face as she stilled his hand. "Let me do this for you. It is why I'm here."

He pulled his hand away. "You want to do this?" Asher asked.

"Yes."

"I will tear up the contract, and you may stay here until we find you a better situation. I will ask nothing else of you. Stay as my guests."

"No. I told you I *could not* agree to that. I've signed the papers, and we have consummated the agreement. I keep my word."

"Are you certain that this is what you want?"

"You keep asking that."

"Because I want you to understand that I respect you enough to make your own decision. That you are free to choose."

"Thank you for showing respect. I am sure about this."

"Then, by all means. Grip it tight. Yes, like that. Now stroke—hard. Do not be gentle." Ash's voice had an agonizing but commanding tone.

Apparently, she had *not* completely satisfied him. So, he retired to his room to see to his gratification? "I was not enough for you? You did not receive any enjoyment rutting me?" Chastity was genuinely curious, for she knew nothing of men's desires.

Ash moaned. "If you only knew what you do to me. Why do you suppose I'm still in this condition?"

Truthfully, his admission should have shocked her. Ash had warned her he possessed an ardent nature. The fact that he confessed she had brought him to such an aroused state thrilled her.

He clasped her hand tight, increasing the pace.

"Faster. Make me come. I want this" —Asher squeezed— "inside you always. Deep. I want to pin you to the bed until we are spent and senseless."

His guttural, erotic speech thrilled her.

My word, does he mean it?

Then why—a hoarse groan left his throat as his climax peaked.

"Damn!" he snarled, backing away from her as he shuddered.

In their few days of acquaintance, she had never seen him this vulnerable and undone. How magnificent he looked standing in the muted moonlight.

Chastity picked up the cloth lying next to the basin and, taking his hand, wiped away the evidence of his desire. His breathing was harsh and uneven.

"You must think me an animal. It's why I left. I did not want to force my base lust on you." Ash shook his head. "And I had planned never to reveal such to you. Yet, I have."

"I'm your mistress. You can unleash your lust if you wish. And speak of it as often as you like," she replied quietly.

"I want to do things with you I have done with no other woman," Ash purred huskily.

Chastity glanced up at him. His golden cognac eyes gleamed with longing. She recognized the look now, and it seized her breath. "You do?"

"From the very moment that I saw you at the ball. While you stood speaking to the other young ladies, I imagined bending you across the nearby settee, rucking up your gown, and thrusting into you. With everyone watching." He shook his head. "And I cannot believe I confessed this secret fantasy to you."

A thrill sparked her senses and caused her heart to flutter. Ash did not frighten her with his frank and sensual talk. It was an unexpected revelation that he stirred a genuine passion in her. "Ash—"

"I pestered my father to arrange an introduction," he continued, interrupting her. "When I finally gained his agreement, we found you'd already gone. I cannot begin to describe the disappointment at the news of your departure. If only I had managed to come sooner. Damn society and decorum. I should have kicked the door down the day after the ball and taken you away."

"You were not to know my fate," Chastity said softly.

"No, I was not to know. But I should not have agreed to employ you as my mistress. No other woman has roused such reactions in me, and because of it, I should not be subjecting you to it. And I am sorry for interrupting you while you tried to speak. Since I am confessing, I wanted to tell you all of it while I had the courage."

She cupped his cheek. Soft whiskers teased her fingers. "I do not mind. It's not a hardship to see to your needs."

Giving her a brief smile, he covered her hand with his.

"But I did not see to your needs at all. Allow me to remedy the situation immediately."

Ash swiped the few items on the table to the floor. He lifted her into his arms and sat her on the surface. Pulling her to the edge, Ash rolled her nightgown past her waist. He dropped to his knees; his intense expression caused prickles of awareness to spark her nerve endings.

Ash nuzzled her inner thigh. "Let me give you pleasure. I want you to come apart under my tongue. I want to taste you, lick you."

Ash's voice, rough with passion, ignited her desire.

Chastity spread her legs wider. "Then, taste me."

Ash dove in and flicked her hardened nub with his wicked tongue. He feasted on every part of her feminine core. Chastity clutched a handful of his silky black hair and guided his thrusts. That incredible feeling built again as if scaling a great height.

Ash glanced up at her. "Feel it? Let yourself fly, Chas. Come for me. Beg me for more."

Chas? Oh, heavens.

Since he looked up at her with such a poignant and passionate gaze, how could she not do as he asked?

"I beg you; I beseech you," she whispered in a husky voice.

Ash groaned at her sensual plea.

A slight smile curved about her lips. It turns out she had begged Ash after all. His response sent sparks up and down her spine.

"What do you desire? Tell me what you want me to do—please." He pleaded. There was no mistaking his tone of voice.

As he said, he would beg as well.

"Lick and taste my—" What should she call it? She often heard the naughty slang but had no idea what to say.

"Quim. Muff. Notch. Cunny. Bloody paradise," Ash offered, his voice hoarse.

She gave him a brilliant smile. "Quim, then."

With a teasing wink, he did as she asked with full enthusiasm, making her tremble. He must enjoy tasting her as he clutched his shaft again, stroking in tandem with the deep plunge of his sinful tongue. Chastity's breathing was fast and uneven.

The more she moaned and writhed on the table, the faster he worked. Spikes of desire shot through her as her release hit. As he'd suggested, she reveled in the new sensations.

Ash groaned and laid his cheek against her thigh as he climaxed.

What would they do now—share a bed? Sleep in each other's arms?

Perhaps after a rest, explore and enjoy each other once again?

The anticipation of continuing and sharing such an intimacy covered her with expectant desire. She was about to speak when Ash stood and turned from her.

"Go to your room, Chastity."

Her blood turned cold.

The imperious lord had returned, and all his heartfelt confessions and proclamations vanished. It was like a switch had been flicked off, and Ash shut down his emotions because he had revealed too much. In their short acquaintance, Chastity had surmised that much about him.

How dare the man?

He dismissed her as one does a servant.

Angry tears clustered on her lashes, but she blinked them away.

She would not show him any emotional response for all the money in the world. She had a stubborn streak a mile wide when the situation called for it.

Fine.

Chastity hopped off the table and lowered her nightgown. "Goodnight, my lord," she replied in a dispassionate tone.

He would not even look at her. As Chastity strode from the room, she made a vow.

Never would she allow him to make her feel anything beyond the carnal.

Ever.

Chapter 9

THE DAY AFTER THEIR passionate encounter, Asher temporarily moved into a few rooms at his club as he said he would. Thankfully, The Rakes of St. Regent's Park kept accommodations at the Albany Street location for such an emergency.

He had to distance himself from the temptation and try and sort out his jumbled thoughts concerning Chastity.

Truthfully, he handled their night together clumsily. Worse, he acted like an unfeeling cad at the end. One feeling besides desire he would acknowledge—guilt.

His foolish plan for staying detached had crumbled to dust. He'd been anything but; his emotions and actions ran the gamut. Losing control and confessing such chaotic feelings was damned embarrassing. And by God, he lost control in all ways. Asher should have stood his ground and declared he had only come into the room to talk. But he did not.

Like a coward, Asher had departed right after sex. He could not face the jumble of emotions tearing through him.

But she came into his room to confront him, nonetheless. Good for her.

Asher was not a complete heel. It was a good deed to remove Chastity and her siblings from the street and give them food, shelter, and other comforts. It was his first thought, after all—to rescue them.

As far as acting on his selfish desires? The lack of control rankled. The mistress arrangement—deemed acceptable in upper-crust society—did not sit well with him. Even though Chastity had suggested it first, deep down, he wanted them to have—what? An affair of the heart? Something with more permanence?

His arrogance disgusted him.

Five days had passed since he'd moved to his club. Asher had stopped by the town house in the afternoons to address his correspondence. They had not shared any meals. Most nights, he had eaten at the club or a nearby pub. God knows what Chastity did to amuse herself, for she remained cloistered in her room.

As he sat nursing a scotch in the club's main meeting room, the door flung open and hit the wall. Damon Cranston, Marquess of Brookton, strolled in.

"I don't usually find you here in the middle of the afternoon, drowning your sorrows?" Damon asked sarcastically.

"And if I am?"

Damon poured scotch into a crystal tumbler and sat at the table opposite. "Then I'll join you. Here's to sorrows." He raised his glass, then threw back a mouthful. "What have to you mope about? You have the world by the tail, you wealthy sod."

"Why bother to explain it? You will make some droll or mocking comments. When have you ever cared about anyone's problems but your own? Perhaps not even then."

Asher wasn't cruel; he spoke the truth and matter-of-factly. Damon had them all beat concerning selfish pleasures and remaining detached in most situations for as long as Asher could recall.

"Ouch. A direct hit. I can be serious enough when the chips are down, old boy. I also can be a damned good listener when I put my mind to it. Go on, tell me your troubles. I am all attention." Damon swiveled toward him at met his gaze. There was no mocking expression visible.

What did he have to lose? Asher told Damon, in general terms, about Chastity and the situation he had found her in. And the fact that she had offered to be his mistress.

"You?" Damon's eyebrows shot up. "A mistress? Isn't that a rather archaic arrangement our grandfathers would make?"

"Not necessarily. Some still follow the practice. And it was the only way she would agree to come with me. That and the promise to look after her siblings. I believe that inducement caused her to suggest the mistress compact in the first place."

Damon shook his head as he reached for the decanter. "Never thought you would be running a charity house. All you had to do was say no."

"I couldn't leave them; they were in dire straits. You should have seen the accommodations they lived in. Utterly deplorable. Three days ago, I stopped in and paid the rent arrears. The landlord is a loathsome bastard. He probably preys on the women tenants. Chastity and her siblings would have perished there; of that, I have no doubt."

Damon shook his head once again. "Mistress or not, you have a past with this young woman regarding unresolved feelings. Is it wise to pull off that scab and subject yourself to heartbreak? Why not give the poor woman a few hundred pounds and send the Armitages on their way? You can well afford it. It will assuage your guilt, and you will do a good deed besides."

He would give Damon his due; he listened to the narrative and offered sound advice. Though he wouldn't exactly agree that he and Chastity had a past, Damon was correct about the unresolved feelings—on his end, at least.

"First off, she would not take the money. I already offered assistance, financial and otherwise. Chastity is proud and wants to earn her way."

"Then put her to work as a maid, or better yet, do so at Wenlock Manor, where Miss Armitage will be tucked away for a time until you sort through your feelings. You can well afford to take on another servant."

"Yes, I can well afford it. But what of Chastity's siblings? And Chastity is not well enough to take on any physical labor. None of them are."

Damon's eyebrows shot upward. "But she is well enough to service you?"

Asher flushed. "I had no control over the situation. It just—happened."

Damon scoffed. "It is not like you to lose control over any situation, which proves you are too far invested in this to make rational decisions. All the more reason to send the Armitage brood to the country, post haste."

Again, it was sound advice. "I don't want Chastity to leave," Asher replied softly.

Damon rolled his eyes. "Christ, not another one. First Christian, now you. You are falling for this street waif, aren't you?"

"Perhaps I am. And don't call her that."

"I apologize."

Which was something Damon rarely did.

"Accepted. As you say, there are unresolved feelings and conflicting emotions. Dismissing Chastity or sending her and her family to Wenlock Manor without exploring these emotions? I would regret it. But beyond my selfishness, the Armitages need to recover. I couldn't turn them out, hundreds of pounds or not." Asher sipped his drink, deciding to change the subject somewhat. "What do you know of Sir Nigel Barrington? He was knighted recently."

"Nothing at all; what do I know of knights? There are hundreds of them. Never heard of the chap."

Asher frowned. "I should dig into his past, see what sort of man would lie, and abandon his guardianship if there is one."

"Why not engage Eleanora Galway?" Damon suggested. "They aren't far from here; I'll send my driver to Cleveland Street, and she can get started immediately."

"The Galway Investigative Agency?"

Damon surprised him again. The agency ladies certainly solved the case Christian had hired them for.

"Yes. The Galway sisters are more than competent. Why not hire them?"

"Very well, send for her."

Damon jumped to his feet and trotted toward the stairs. He returned in a manner of minutes.

"He's off. Meanwhile, let's have another drink."

Close to ten minutes later, Althea Galway, Eleanora's younger sister and partner in the agency entered the room.

Damon's shoulders immediately stiffened, his cheeks flushing a bright crimson. Asher recalled what Christian had recently said about Damon being interested in Althea. Here lay the proof. He had never seen Damon react to any woman before in this way, showing an interest, rattled at her presence.

Asher stood and held out his hand. "Miss Galway. Are you alone?"

She took his hand and shook it. "Wenlock, it's nice to see you. Eleanora and Sybil are out on a divorce case, but I'm available." She glanced toward Damon. "Don't get up on my account, Brookton."

"I wasn't planning on it. At any rate, Miss Galway, nice to see you," he replied tartly.

Then he did the strangest thing. Damon jumped to his feet, gave her an exaggerated bow, then pulled out her chair.

"May I offer you a drink, Miss Galway?" he asked.

"No, thank you," she replied curtly.

By God, Christian was correct, Damon *was* interested, and the awareness was returned. Asher could swear sparks were flying between the couple.

Once seated, he told the story Chastity had revealed, what little of it there was.

Miss Galway pulled out a notebook and pencil and took notes. "Miserable man, taking advantage of orphans, and in the worst possible way," Miss Galway tsked as she wrote. "What would you like me to discover? If this Barrington has legal guardianship over the brother and sister? I assume Miss Chastity is past the legal coming of age."

"Yes, she is now. And anything you can find about Barrington, including the guardianship question and if her mother left a will," Asher replied.

"I'll get started right away." She stood, gathering her notebook and pencil.

Damon pulled out a roll of pound notes and peeled off several. "How much, Miss Galway, for a retainer? Ten pounds? Twenty?"

"Listen," Asher interjected. "This is my case; I—"

But Miss Galway held up her hand. "For you, my lord marquess, the price is forty. But as the baron said, it's his case. For him, the price is ten to start."

Damon chuckled as he tucked his money away.

Asher paid her.

"Where do you wish me to send word?" Miss Galway asked as she tucked the pound notes into her reticule.

Asher handed her his card. "My town house, you have the address. My butler, Grimes, is the man to talk to if I am not there. He will send word to me, and we can set up a meeting."

"Allow me to escort you to the carriage, Miss Galway." Damon gave her another sweeping bow.

"Stop mocking me," she barked irritably. "And I will walk; it's not that far. I don't need or want your escort."

Miss Galway whirled about and marched toward the door but stumbled.

Asher had never seen Damon move so fast. He grasped her arm, keeping her from falling.

"Do you only lose your footing in my presence, I wonder? Do I affect you that much, Miss Galway? Remember, this happened before, in your parlor."

The lady detective's face flushed. "Release me," she muttered crossly. But Damon didn't.

Asher folded his arms and leaned against the wall, fascinated by the exchange. And the heat they generated. Sparks indeed.

"Althea," Damon said, his voice serious. All vestiges of the sardonic rake had disappeared. "Please take the carriage. And as a favor to me, to both of us," he pointed at Asher. "I have a smaller carriage. Use it as you investigate this case. It will be at your disposal. And you should see a doctor. You are not steady on your feet."

Asher waited for Althea to snap at Damon and admonish him, but she didn't. The young lady lingered, leaning against Damon. Several moments passed, and Asher wondered if he should quit the room to give them privacy.

Then, she stepped away from him.

"I do appreciate your concern, but I am perfectly fine. Good day, gentlemen."

Damon stood at the top of the stairs, watching her until she exited the building. "Perfectly fine, indeed," he whispered.

"What is going on, Damon?" Asher called out.

Damon whirled around as if he had forgotten Asher was still there.

"Mind your business," he snarled as he marched to the bar. Grasping the whiskey decanter, he splashed a generous amount into a tumbler.

"You listened to my troubles, allow me to return the favor," Asher said as he joined Damon at the counter.

"I have no troubles."

Asher chuckled as he filled his glass. "You could have ignited a forest fire with the heat the two of you engendered."

"It is of no matter." Damon threw back his drink and poured another. "I cannot act on it. No more than you can act on your own runaway blaze. They are not suitable matches, either young lady. According to so-called society." Damon spat out the last word.

"That didn't stop Christian."

Damon snorted. "He is already a duke and can do as he pleases. I, however, will have any match I care to make closely scrutinized and approved by my intractable and loathsome duke father. Althea would never pass muster. Not that I am considering any match with anyone at all. I prefer my bachelor status."

"I suppose I can do as I please as well. My father is no longer among the living to pass judgment, not that he ever would have. Nor would the exalted upper crust give a hang what a baron does."

"Aren't you lucky," Damon said drolly.

"Lucky is correct. My father wasn't horrible at all. Certainly not what The Rakes have dealt with—or dealing with. I think you are using your father as an excuse—"

Damon slammed his empty glass on the bar. "I believe I will seek out some female company. Care to join me? Oh, wait. You have your own private concubine squirreled away."

And here it is.

Damon often stirred the pot when emotions came into play. He had acted this way ever since they were boys. Asher would not indulge him, though Damon deserved a punch in the face for that crass comment concerning Chastity. Damon, knowing he had revealed far too much, lashed out.

"Have a care, Brookton. As usual, you go too far. Then off you go on your empty adventures. Good day to you."

Summarily dismissed, Damon strolled from the room, leaving Asher more confused, for he had resolved nothing, despite the excellent advice from Damon.

One thing at a time. Find out what was going on with the Armitages' legal standing.

Perhaps then he could examine his swirling emotions and try to make sense of them.

Chapter 10

Grimes had reported to Asher that Chastity had taken a tray into her room and that the children had taken their meal in the schoolroom with the new governess. Chastity's brother and sister kept to the rooms in the attic and the sitting room on the third floor.

Since the first night they'd arrived, Asher had no contact with the younger Armitages. But then, why would he? He trusted his staff to see to their proper care.

Miss Elizabeth Tallen, the middle-aged governess, had settled in and immediately engaged the children in furthering their schooling. The woman had been a fortunate find. Grimes gave him regular reports concerning the children's education, but the time had come for Asher to speak to the governess and inspect the schoolroom.

Not that there had ever been a schoolroom in this residence. His father had bought this town house after his mother died because he could no longer bear to live at Wenlock Manor. The late baron had also sold their London residence for the same reason. The memories were too painful. Asher could understand it. At least here, no ghostly childhood memories were lurking in dark corners. Not that he had any horrible memories, unlike others in his acquaintance. Watford and Brookton came to mind, though he wasn't aware of all the details.

Asher tossed aside his letters and newspapers and exited the study. Enough speculating about the children; it was time to investigate the matter. Standing outside the schoolroom, he heard animated young voices. Without knocking, Asher opened the door and stepped across the threshold.

The chatter ceased, and the two children and governess turned to face him. Miss Tallen stood as the young girl, Hannah, smiled prettily and gave him an adorably awkward curtsy.

"Good afternoon, your lordship," the girl said.

Asher bowed. "And good afternoon to you, Miss Hannah."

A sunny smile broke across her face, and he gave her one in return. The lad remained seated, giving him a scorching gaze of contempt. Asher raised an eyebrow at the disrespectful stare.

Instead of reacting, Asher turned his attention to the governess. She possessed a kind and pleasant face, which in Asher's view, was of paramount importance. Threads of gray intermingled with the brownish-black shade of her hair. Her tight-knot hairstyle and the gray wool gown she wore completed the standard governess look.

Miss Tallen smiled. "Good afternoon, my lord. I am very pleased you could join us." She turned her gaze to Jon, and the smile slipped away. "Master Jon," she said firmly, "Stand and greet his lordship."

Jon's eyes narrowed. Asher could see the lad struggling with defying the governess's authority. Sneering, he pushed back his chair, the legs scraping along the wood floor. He stood with his eyes cast down and shoulders hunched forward in disrespect.

"Good afternoon—*my lord.*"

The last two words were spat out, the venom plain.

The governess sputtered, but Asher held his hand up and shook his head. There was no use admonishing the boy further; it would only deepen the scorn apparent in Jon's speech and comportment. Yes, it was best to ignore the insolence.

"Please, be seated," Asher asked. The governess and the children took their seats. "Tell me, Miss Tallen, how do you find your students? Feel free to say whatever you wish. I am sure Jon and Hannah are most eager to hear your assessment."

He gave Hannah a playful wink, and she smiled once again. One day she would be as beautiful as her older sister. Asher caught derision in the lad's expression from the corner of his eye.

"Both children are bright and intelligent. Hannah shows great promise in arts and music, and Jon possesses a keen mind and understanding of everything around him."

Jon shifted uncomfortably in his seat, flushing with embarrassment at the praise. Did a slight smile curl about the lad's mouth? Jon was pleased by the governess's compliment.

"Is that right?" Asher stood next to Jon's desk, then tapped the open book. "What are you studying?"

Jon looked away, effectively ignoring him.

"Jon, you will answer his lordship immediately!" Miss Tallen cautioned.

Asher grabbed a chair and pulled it over to sit next to him. "You do not have to like me, Jon. But in this schoolroom, you will show respect in your sister's and Miss Tallen's presence, even if it is toward me. I am *not* the enemy. Now, tell me what you're studying."

Moisture gathered in Jon's eyes; then, he cleared his throat. "I'm studying Latin, my lord." The voice was cool but steady.

"An interesting and ancient language, certainly needed for further higher education. Well met, Jon. I have numerous Latin and Ancient Greek books if those topics interest you. Feel free to borrow any book you wish."

Jon turned to face him. "I can borrow any book?" His eyes widened, and a slow smile crept across his face. Then, as if remembering to whom he spoke, the smile disappeared, and an impassive expression returned.

Asher stood. "Of course, you may. I would extend the invitation to you, Hannah, but I doubt you would find anything you would like in the library. Inform Miss Tallen what books you prefer, and I will see they are purchased."

"Oh, thank you, my lord!" Hannah beamed.

"I will leave you to your studies."

Asher turned toward Miss Tallen. In a lower voice, he said, "Whatever you need for their education, please inform Grimes. We will spare no expense."

"I will. Thank you, my lord," the governess replied.

Asher stood by the door and clasped the handle. "Hannah and Jon. I wish you both to join me for dinner tonight. I will inform your sister of the details." He bowed. "Good afternoon."

Hannah called out a response, but Jon said nothing. Shaking his head, Asher stepped into the hall and closed the door behind him. He couldn't fault the lad for his disrespect, for he was old enough to understand the arrangement with Chastity. Whatever this situation was. What started as a ruse had moved into an actual mistress compact, which was not his intent. But Asher had allowed his emotions to cloud his judgment. The utter scorn in Jon's eyes added to his guilt concerning this entire situation.

This was not working out the way Asher thought it would. He wasn't supposed to care about Chastity and her family. They were only to stay here briefly, recovering while he investigated ways to improve their circumstances.

But he did.

And he was not sure what to do about it.

CHASTITY SAT IN HER room as she had done the previous five afternoons. A small fire snapped and crackled in the hearth. Since she could not sew or embroider, she had little to occupy herself. While she had borrowed books from Ash's library, and as much as she enjoyed Dickens, Trollope, and revisiting the works of Jane Austen, she could not concentrate on reading.

Absently, she fingered a wayward tendril of hair. All of them had their hair cut the day after they'd arrived.

"Luckily, you don't have lice," Anna, the maid, had commented when snipping the dry and uneven ends.

Still, they had fleas on their clothes. No wonder Ash had ordered their few possessions burned, including their meager wardrobes. Chastity had not been sorry to see the frayed clothes destroyed. She wished she could also toss the horrid memories of the last couple of years in the fireplace. They would not be easy to destroy. Every morning she awoke, Chastity could swear she was back in that drafty room, and a feeling of dread would overtake her—until she got her bearings and realized she was at Lord Ash's town house. But for how long? Chastity couldn't dwell on the unknown. All that mattered was that her brother and sister were safe for now. Honestly, they needed to recover, both physically and emotionally. Chastity was well aware that they all suffered severe trauma, and it could not be dismissed lightly.

Not only could she not concentrate on reading, but sleep had become impossible even though the bed was comfortable and warm. She lay there early in the evenings listening to Ash on the other side of the connecting door moving about his room.

The stubborn man was as restless as she, but Chastity couldn't bring herself to knock on the door. Stubborn pride had kept her in her room. Then she'd hear him depart for his club, or perhaps to another woman, not to return until later in the afternoon.

This situation had grown intolerable.

It had been over a week since Chastity's intimate encounter with Ash. Or any encounter at all, if it came to that. She relived their sensual rendezvous over and over in her mind. It had been fraught with intense emotions on both sides with powerful but unnamed feelings, at least on her part. She also wondered why Lord Ash had turned cold and unyielding.

Chastity sighed. What did she know of affairs, mistresses, and the proper decorum involved in such an arrangement?

Did she mistake what passed between them? Quite possibly.

Regardless of the two brief tups she'd endured on the streets, Chastity never dreamed she could experience such passion.

Was it always as such?

After observing the bored look on the prossies' faces in Shag Alley, she rather doubted it. Perhaps her expectations were so low that what occurred between them heightened and intensified.

Chastity closed her eyes and recalled how wantonly she sat on the table, legs spread, Ash kneeling at her feet. There was no doubt that she wanted him between her legs again—her eyes popped open. She shuddered with yearning.

What in heaven's name was the matter with her?

A soft tap at the door interrupted her heated thoughts.

"Chastity? May I come in?"

Oh no, Ash.

Her insides quivered with expectation at the sound of his deep, melodic voice. Chastity reached for her shawl and pulled it around her shoulders.

Exhaling on a shaky breath, she fought to gain control of her wayward emotions. "Yes. Come in, my lord."

Ash closed the door behind him. His presence was intoxicating, as always. His afternoon suit fit as well as all the other clothing he wore. Knowing what masculine perfection lay underneath the black wool made him vastly appealing. Heat rushed to her cheeks. Blast her reaction. She could hide nothing of her feelings.

"I've just visited your siblings. They appear to be thriving," he stated.

Why would he bother with my brother and sister?

She could think of nothing to say.

Ash stepped closer, motioning to the chair across from hers. "May I sit?"

"Of course."

He lowered himself into the leather wing chair and crossed his long legs. "Will you share your experiences of the past few years?"

Chastity frowned. "Why? Do you wish to be entertained?"

Ash rubbed his temple and blew out an exasperated breath. "Of course, your tragic tale would amuse me to no end. I revel in your downfall. God, Chastity! What sort of man do you think I am?" His voice raised in sarcastic annoyance.

"I don't *know* what kind of man you are, my lord. How am I to recognize what amuses a man who has been handed everything on silver and lives for his selfish gratifications?" she snapped.

Ash shook his head. "I have experienced loss. Both my parents are dead. Not everything has been as easy or smooth as you believe. As for my gratifications—"

"There has been a multitude of willing women, I've no doubt," Chastity interrupted crossly. Why was she acting petulant? It was none of her concern how many past paramours Ash had enjoyed.

Ash glowered. "You wish for me to share my experiences? Not a problem. I have a plethora of sexual adventures to draw upon, considering my membership in the Rakes of St. Regent's Park."

"I've heard of your group," Chastity replied flatly. "You are the talk of the streets. Your reputation proceeds you."

"I can well imagine. I will let you in on a little secret. As of late, we are not quite the lecherous libertines as you might suppose. At least, I am not."

"As of late? But in your past—"

"We can swap tales and regale each other into the wee hours. Yes, there have been several women, but I've never had a long-term association with them nor made any of them my mistress. I do not make of habit of bringing strangers into my home."

"Then, why me?" Chastity whispered.

He turned and looked at her, confusion plain in his expression. "I have no earthly idea. Are you telling me you've had a change of heart? I have the signed contract on my desk." Ash pointed in the direction of his study.

"Bought and paid for. I'm aware of the contract. I will see it through." She replied, her voice aloof. "I suppose you will be waving that document under my nose at every opportunity to gain what you want, like some obedient spaniel waiting for instructions from the all-powerful master."

Chastity's annoyance lay beyond all logic as she was the one who proposed this situation and initiated it. How gullible of her to think emotion would not enter into this.

Ash waved his hand dismissively. "I have no intention of holding the contract over your head or under your nose, and I know nothing of spaniels. I've never owned one. Besides, becoming my mistress was *your* idea, if you recall."

"And the contract was yours."

It is you who insisted on this mistress compact. "It was done to protect and ensure you receive good benefits and compensation. I also offered to rip it to shreds and have you and your siblings stay here as my guests. I only agreed to it so that you would come with me."

Well, he had her there. Chastity had insisted on it. "You truly didn't wish for this arrangement?"

"All I wanted was to assist you and your family. It was my primary aim, I swear it. Matters took on a life of their own."

"Yes, it did. We lost our heads. I wanted the contract, truth be told. To gain stability for myself and my brother and sister, even if only for a few months. In my mind, securing a future for us, especially my brother and sister, pushed away all other considerations. I am sorry."

"For what?"

"I was entirely too pushy about it. Desperation makes a person do things they normally wouldn't do. Or say or suggest things they normally would never say or suggest. But nothing has been normal these past few years."

As in making the mistress offer, to begin with.

Ash's look softened at her confession. "I wanted to offer assistance in any way that I could. If that meant agreeing to your mistress demand, then so be it. Just because we agreed to such an arrangement does not mean we must stick to it. Think about it. We can make any variations you wish."

Chastity nodded.

"Allow me to change the subject momentarily," Ash continued. "I'm here to extend an invitation to dinner tonight for all of you. Dinner will be at seven in the dining room. I have already invited Hannah and Jon, and they've accepted."

"Why? What are you doing?" Chastity clasped the shawl tighter, her emotions swirling in a confused state.

This man caused her insides to reel. Honestly, she hadn't stood on solid ground since they met. Not that her life was all that stable before.

"I will not have us occupy this house like strangers."

"We have certainly been strangers the past several nights."

He arched a thick eyebrow. "Indeed? Are you inviting me to your room, to your bed? Have you missed my attentions? I thought to give you a reprieve."

She eyed him askance. "Why do you keep saying that? You seem to have more of a problem with your beastly lust than I do. And those were your words, not mine."

Ash frowned once again. He didn't speak for several moments. "You may be right. I will return to live here shortly. I need a little more time."

"For what?"

"To work out what is going on between us. I want to know you better. Can we forgo the physical aspect and concentrate on becoming better acquainted?"

Chastity did not understand what was going on.

The emotions from both of them ran the gamut from irritability to impatience. Did all physical relations have such capricious undertones? How tempting to ask why he needed to distance himself from her. Doing so would imply that she cared, and she didn't want to reveal her feelings any more than she already had.

"I don't see what that would accomplish."

"Accomplish? I just said I don't want us to be strangers; I cannot be much plainer than that. Say so now if you would rather be an employee and nothing else. I can have Mrs. Grimes find you work." Ash shook his head. "Forget I said that. I am not usually so petulant."

"I will forget it for now. I don't want us to be indifferent strangers, but I also do not think forming any attachment is wise." Or so she told herself. "I will do as you ask. We shall become acquainted, then. It is as good a place as any to start."

Ash frowned, not happy with her response, judging by the annoyed look on his face.

"I do not wish to argue with you about any of this. We should change the subject once again. One thing we need to discuss is Barrington's status, legally speaking. What can you tell me?"

Chastity pulled at the fringe of her shawl. "I know Mother left a will, though I don't know the contents. All the solicitor told me of the will was Sir Nigel would be our legal guardian."

"Why in hell would your mother do such a thing?"

Exasperation rolled through her. "I told you. Sir Nigel kept his unscrupulous interest in us well hidden. My mother had no idea of his intent. It was after Mother passed that he showed his true colors. Until then, he treated us with polite indifference. There was no one else to look after us. Were we to be taken to an orphanage, then? Or maybe the workhouse?"

"You would have been better off!" Ash exclaimed.

"Better apart? No. Never. I vowed to protect Jon and Hannah and solemnly promised we would *never* be separated. I kept my word. And do you even know what awaits in those places? God knows where we would have wound up or what fate had in store. At least together, we had a chance."

"Are you even aware of your horrible circumstances? You all could have died in a month or two, weeks even!" Ash cried.

"And are *you* aware just how many people are in those horrible circumstances? Do you even care?" Chastity shouted.

The ticking of the mantel clock was the only sound in the room. She had gone too far.

"I care about *you;* that's a start," Ash replied, his voice quiet.

"And I thank you for it." She meant it; Chastity was eternally grateful for his rescue.

"Regarding Sir Nigel. How old were you when you ran that night?"

"Twenty. But I am twenty-three now, liberated from Sir Nigel."

"But not free from me, you mean. You are not a prisoner, nor am I keeping you here hostage!" Ash slammed his fist on the arm of the chair and then exhaled.

"What is going on between us?" Chastity whispered.

"It is fraught with emotions that we are having trouble grappling with. I apologize for the show of temper. Regardless, one thing to remember: Jon and Hannah are *not* free from Sir Nigel. They are his wards until they reach the age of majority. Lawfully speaking, they can be returned to him."

"No! It's why we fled. You know what he will do, what they will be subjected to." Her voice shook as tears spilled down her cheeks.

Oh, drat it!

She buried her face in her hands and sobbed.

Chastity was surprised by a sudden masculine embrace. Ash had gently pulled her out of her chair and into his arms. Sniffling, she lay against Ash's chest, the wool of his coat scraping her cheeks.

He tucked her head under his chin and stroked her hair, whispering words of comfort. "There, Chas. Here is further proof that we are having difficulties reigning in our emotions. Please, do not despair. I will see my solicitor, Mr. Peebles, to see what can be done."

He stepped back, his arms still about her in a sheltering and gentle hold. He chucked her lightly under the chin. "You are *not* my hostage. You must know I would do anything to protect you," Ash stated, his voice tender. "And in turn, I will protect your brother and sister. I will not see them returned to that miserable bastard. You have my word."

She cried out with relief and threw her arms around his neck. How desperately she wanted to believe him. How well could one come to know another person in a matter of days?

Chastity must take him at his word, or at least try to, as no one else could assist them. The ability to trust another fled three years ago.

Without thinking, Chastity laid a firm kiss on his lips. A low, guttural groan left Ash's throat as he pulled her closer and kissed her wildly. As quickly as the kiss overwhelmed her, it ended in moments. As he stated, their emotions were running amuck.

Ash backed away until he reached behind him for the doorknob.

"See you at dinner promptly at seven."

As he disappeared into the hall, Chastity touched her lips which still ached from the passionate kiss.

Remaining indifferent became difficult the more she was in his presence.

Chapter 11

AFTER MEETING WITH Chastity, Asher grabbed his greatcoat, called for his carriage, and traveled toward Mr. Peebles's office.

All the way there, he went over their emotionally charged encounter. They sniped at each other; as if not wishing to fully acknowledge the breadth and depth of the intense feelings passing between them. There were so many emotions that he could not separate them in his muddled mind.

No woman ever had him so unmoored as this.

One smart thing he proposed was halting the physical aspect, as it only complicated matters until he had a handle on what he was feeling, no sex. And no more heated kisses.

Upon arriving at his solicitor's office, he was ushered inside. Luckily, Mr. Peebles was free of appointments and could see him immediately. Asher explained the particulars of the Armitages' predicament to the solicitor.

Adjusting his spectacles, Peebles cleared his throat and said, "With the Guardianship of Infants Act in 1886, women have the right to be made the sole guardian of their children when their husbands died."

"They didn't before?"

"Not at all, my lord. Legally speaking, women were not considered a separate being apart from their husbands until the Married Women's Property Act of 1884. All this should have happened long before this."

"I agree, Mr. Peebles. Do all these long-overdue rights mean a woman could make her own will, unbeknownst to her new husband?"

"Highly unlikely, as barely fifteen percent of the British population make wills. But beyond that, and regardless of improvements in women's rights, Mrs. Barrington could not have filed a will without Sir Nigel's consent and full knowledge of the contents. Such are the laws governing female wills, my lord."

Though Asher made periodic appearances at Parliament in the House of Lords, this could be one debate of judicial reasoning he could get behind: furthering the rights of children and women. No one should have to take to the streets to escape a calamitous circumstance. Chastity had no legal recourse.

"Unless she made provisions regarding the children while a widow," Mr. Peebles added. "Then she would not have had to let her new husband be aware of any existing will."

"According to the oldest sibling, Chastity, Sir Nigel was given guardianship of the children until they came of age. What is that, twenty-one?" Asher asked.

"Yes, it is."

"Well, Chastity passed that age now, but legally speaking, the two younger children are under the guardianship of Sir Nigel."

"That is correct, my lord."

"What can you tell me about the guardianship laws?"

"Generally, the children are wards of Sir Nigel, legally considered possessions. With their mother's death, they became orphans. A guardian is authorized to hold and manage the property of the minors in question."

Asher crossed his arms, frowning. "As far as I am aware, Mrs. Barrington brought nothing to her marriage to Sir Nigel except her offspring. No property or monies of any kind, according to Chastity. It is why she married; the family was in terrible financial straits, as I've explained."

So why did Sir Nigel marry Mrs. Armitage?

She must have been attractive if her appearance was similar to the children's. The poor woman, no doubt, had to take the first offer of matrimony since no male relatives existed for protection.

"If she held no assets, why make a will?" Asher questioned.

Peebles scratched his beard. "It must concern the children exclusively. With no relatives or family friends to turn to, she had no one *but* Sir Nigel to name as guardian. Or so we can assume."

"I have hired the Galway Investigative Agency. They have been tasked with investigating Sir Nigel and determining whether any wills or custody arrangements exist. I wish you to look into any legal paths as well."

"I will do my best, my lord."

"Althea Galway will soon be in touch. If and when we find any such agreement and ascertain the contents, we can formulate a plan. What plan, I have no idea."

"Has Miss Armitage the elder ever seen any agreement, my lord?"

Asher shook his head. "No. She only had Sir Nigel's stating of the fact. He also had his attorney repeat it. Chastity does not remember the name of the solicitor, unfortunately."

"Let us assume there is a legal document. Taking this case to court could take months, years even. In the interim, the children could feasibly be returned to Sir Nigel or become wards of the court. The sordid reasons for a change in guardianship will be made public. It would be the children's word against a knight of the realm. The squalid and sensational story would make all the papers."

"Not the route I wish to pursue."

"Completely understandable. Leave it with me, my lord. I shall await Miss Galway's getting in touch, and in the interim, I will do a little investigating of my own. You see, guardians must submit a statement to the court annually to renew their bonds."

"Bonds?" Ash questioned. Good lord, he had no idea the laws were so complicated. Children considered as possessions? It was inhuman. But until recently, women were considered the same.

"Yes, my lord. When Sir Nigel agreed to be guardian, he had to take an oath and post a bond, which varies in amount regarding the estate. Since there was no money or property for the Armitage children, the bond amount would be a pittance but needed before he was given a letter of guardianship."

"I had no idea it was so complex."

"Since 1868, these agreements must be recorded with the court. I will try and find out what I can," Mr. Peebles stated.

Asher stood and held out his hand. Mr. Pebbles took it. "Thank you. I am glad you are so well versed in the area of law. I can rely on your discretion as always."

"Of course, my lord."

Exiting the office and heading toward his carriage, Asher decided to drop in on Christian. He needed counsel of a personal nature.

ASHER WAS SHOWN INTO Christian Bamford's study and told that Eleanora Galway would join him presently. It appeared Eleanora spent much time here with Christian, and Asher couldn't be happier for them.

Asher could see why Damon was attracted to Eleanora's sister, Althea. She had the same determined and confident aura as her older sister. Asher imagined Althea would not take any nonsense from Damon. But many obstacles lay between them, perhaps too many to allow any significant attachment. Time will tell.

Eleanora entered, wearing a copper-colored tea gown, looking every inch the duchess-to-be. She held out her hand, and Asher took it, kissing lightly across her knuckles.

"How good it is to see you, Wenlock," she said, smiling warmly.

"Asher, please. We are to be friends, are we not?"

She motioned toward the sofa, and she sat in the nearby chair. "Of course. Asher. Friends indeed. Shall I ring for tea? Or would you prefer a drink, though I suppose it is early?"

"Tea would be welcome. This is not entirely a social call."

Eleanora rose and rang the buzzer, then took her seat. "I wondered. Christian is still lazing about upstairs; he will be down directly."

In other words, they had been in bed.

The corner of Asher's mouth quirked. "Sorry to disturb you."

Eleanora chuckled. "It was time we were up and about anyway."

A maid entered. "You rang, Miss Galway?"

"Yes. Tea for three and a few sandwiches and sweets wouldn't go amiss. Thank you, Doris."

The maid departed, and Eleanora shook her head. "I still cannot get used to all this upper-crust business. I'm entirely out of my element. But I am adjusting. So, do tell me what brings you here. An investigative inquiry? The one you hired Althea for?"

"You guessed correctly. You have more work than you can handle, I hear. Althea offered to take on the assignment."

Since The Rakes case, the one that brought Christian and Eleanora together, word had spread far and wide of the fearless ladies of the agency. The business had picked up enough that the sisters were considering taking on another employee.

"But I am here regarding a personal matter as well," Asher added.

"Would you rather speak to Christian alone? I should have asked."

"Not at all. As you said, we are friends. Stay, by all means."

The maid entered with the tea tray, placed it on the table before Eleanora, and departed.

Soon after, Christian strolled into the room. "Asher, this is a pleasant surprise."

Once he sat beside Eleanora, Christian affectionately kissed her cheek and took the cup and saucer she held toward him.

"What do we owe this pleasure?" Christian said as he sipped his tea.

"I'll get right to it."

Asher explained finding Chastity, following her to her room, and discovering her siblings. Her mistress suggestion and his agreement to it and the reasons why. Obviously, he didn't give details of their physical encounters, merely alluding that they had one. Asher also explained about Sir Nigel and why the Armitages ran for their lives.

Eleanora slammed her cup on the tray. "Damn that man for abusing their trust and preying on their innocence. No wonder Miss Armitage departed so hastily; I don't blame her. I also admire her for keeping her family together for nearly three years. My God. That must have been dreadful. Life on the streets is perilous. I have seen it firsthand."

"Yes, dreadful and worse than she is letting on. My dormant and intense feelings returned when I saw her outside the alley. Not that they ever left, it seems. Not only desire but an overwhelming need to protect her. But from what? She had already experienced the worst life has to offer." Asher exhaled. "She certainly stood up to me, making her demands to secure protection for her siblings. Chastity is stubborn. If I hadn't agreed, she wouldn't have come with me. And now-now—"

"You don't want such an agreement between you. You want Chastity Armitage to stay with you for reasons other than protection or a contract," Eleanora interjected gently. "I must say I find this notion of mistresses and contracts abhorrent. But I can imagine Miss Armitage believed it to be the only way to ensure the immediate safety of her brother and sister."

"Yes, you have the right of it. I find the notion abhorrent as well. This situation has me all at sea. Confusion doesn't even begin to describe what is happening inside me," Asher lamented.

Christian and Eleanora exchanged knowing looks.

"Well, with recent experience in some of what you're feeling, allow me to illuminate. You are falling in love with her, Asher. There is nothing else for it," Christian stated firmly.

Asher slowly nodded. "Yes, I believe you are correct. I am certainly falling."

"You were wise to pull the breaks on any further physical encounters," Christian said.

Eleanora nodded. "Miss Armitage has been traumatized; she needs time to heal. And you are offering that time. This trauma no doubt fueled her shocking request. Your job is to convince her that this contract is not binding, that you never wanted it, and that she is free to embrace her feelings. You said she kissed you enthusiastically; that is a good start." Eleanora stated. "She is not indifferent to you."

An image of Chastity with her head back, moaning passionately as he feasted on her, filled his mind.

"No. Not indifferent at all."

Eleanora held out the teapot and refilled Asher's cup. "I will assist Althea in her investigation. I will make time."

"Thank you, Eleanora. Thank you both for listening."

"What are friends for?" Christian smiled.

Thank God he had such friends, for they had put things succinctly enough for him to grapple with. It also showed that he had handled this clumsily from the very start, allowing his rampant emotions to rule over all common sense.

There was no mistake about it.

He was falling for her.

Strictly speaking, those intense emotions never left him. Asher became adept at hiding them. He believed he would never again experience such a swift and potent response to a woman.

But he had. And it was the exact same young lady that had stirred up those feelings before.

Life was strange, indeed.

Chapter 12

HOURS LATER, WATSON, his valet, held up his formal dinner jacket, and Asher slipped his arms through the sleeves. After straightening the grain across his shoulders, Watson swept the coat with a brush and stepped back.

"Do you require anything else, my lord?"

"No, Watson. Thank you."

The valet bowed and exited the room.

Asher stood before the full-length mirror; the reflection showed an adequate specimen.

Up to this point, his life unfolded according to his well-thought-out plan. After his father's death, he became Baron Wenlock and carried on much as before concerning his profligate pursuits. There was a time for settling down, and seeing to an heir would be considered when he turned thirty-three. At least, that is the age he had picked some years ago. Who knows why he had pulled that particular age out of his hat? There were three years to live as he pleased—if he stuck to that asinine plan.

The baron title originated in the 16th century, so he knew the importance of duty, heirs, and family. Asher had assumed he would not have difficulty procuring a suitable bride being a member of the aristocracy and wealthy, even if he stood on the bottom rung of the peerage ladder. He had not been sentimental enough to wish for a love match. What his parents had shared was rare.

In truth, he would have settled for an agreement of mutual benefit, visited his wife's bed chambers until he had the heir and a spare, and retired his family to the country while he resided in the city. Many in the peerage lived this type of life and had for decades.

Which brought his thoughts right back to Chastity.

How she made his blood fire. And his heart soar.

What *if* she stayed on as his mistress?

If he wished to keep her independent from his life as Baron Wenlock, he would have to purchase a separate dwelling for Chastity and her siblings far distant from Mayfair and London society. Isn't that the done thing when it comes to mistresses?

Asher frowned at his reflection in the mirror. Could he accept such a cold arrangement? Could he be as callous as all that? Why did the thought even cross Asher's mind? The arrogance to even consider it hypothetically. The revelation did not sit well with him. He dismissed it once and for all. He was weary of all this inner reflection, but how else was he to sort through his muddled emotions? Ignoring it was not an option.

Did he wish to have the vacuous, monotonous life of an aristocrat? Disconnected and removed from all emotion and compassion? He had tried to act the part when out with his friends, but his heart was not in it. Not of late.

Hell, he tried to act the part with Chastity—so far, it had been a dismal failure.

Why deny it?

Chastity stirred him as no other woman before. He wanted her with a fierceness that belayed all common sense. Setting her aside had only stirred up the embers more.

Asher came to the swift conclusion that he did not want the stuffy, empty life of a bored and emotionless aristocrat.

He wanted what Christian and Eleanora had.

A loving, passionate friendship and partnership. The way they had seamlessly meshed their divergent lives was to be admired.

Why couldn't he have—and do—the same? Especially the passionate part.

Closing his eyes, he imagined Chastity wearing a gold corset accentuating her plump breasts. Matching stockings would complete the picture, her golden-brown hair loose about her shoulders. Asher wanted to feed her lobster pâté on delicate pastries. Take a fine Madeira and pour it over her naked breasts, lick and suck as much of the wine as he could while the rest trailed down her luscious torso like a stream after a spring rain. He wanted the wine to soak the curling, coffee-colored hair of her quim. Follow the cascade with his tongue, lapping eagerly while the rich taste of the wine mixed with her honey sweetness.

Devour, drink. Possess.

Asher groaned as his cock stiffened at the visualization. Despite his sensual daydream, there was more at play. Regardless of his erotic imaginings, he longed to protect and hold her to his heart. Ensure that nothing ever harmed her or her loved ones ever again.

Guard her with his last dying breath.

With sudden and swift clarity, he admitted what he had tried years to deny. Desire was not the only thing that had violently seized him in that damned ballroom close to three years past. It had been infatuation at first sight, more than anything. But from that grew more complicated emotions.

Love at first sight, then?

That was the stuff of fictional plays and novels. Yet, those complex feelings had gripped Asher tight. It still did. He loved her with such an intense yearning that his insides ached. Christian was right; Asher had fallen in love. Again, with the same woman.

But would she ever feel the same toward him?

CHASTITY, JON, AND Hannah awaited Ash's appearance in the dining room. Two footmen stood nearby, ready to serve from the silver chafing dishes on the sideboard.

Never had Chastity seen such a table.

Two elaborately lit candelabras adorned each end of the setting, casting a golden, magical glow. Elegant white, gold-trimmed china and crystal goblets added to the grace of the room. Chastity absently fingered one of the silver spoons. This was beyond her knowledge and entirely too formal for her limited experience. There were too many utensils.

A bleak reminder that Ash lived in a stratum far above hers.

Her dress was the best of the secondhand ones currently in her possession. While taking her seat, she realized the light blue frock fit too snugly through her bosom. Her cleavage was displayed more enticingly than she wished.

Turning her attention from her risqué gown, she glanced worriedly at Hannah. Her sister was still pale, thin, and recovering from her recent chest congestion. Already her siblings looked better, even with one week of steady, healthy eating. Perhaps in a month or two, they would all be nearly recovered. Lord Ash had been right on one point; they were close to perishing. Chastity could admit that now.

Her sister also wore a blue gown, but one more befitting her young age. In the past, it was often said she and Hannah looked alike, though Hannah's hair was lighter than her own.

Jon sat next to Hannah with his arms crossed in defiance. Smartly dressed in a waistcoat and jacket far too big for him, she wondered if they were Ash's castoffs. Her brother made it plain that he wanted to be anywhere than sharing dinner with the baron.

The baron entered the room. Had she ever seen a man who could wear clothes as well? He wore a black dinner suit, and the only color visible was the white cravat tied smartly at his throat. He looked entirely confident and—handsome. Ash acknowledged the footmen's bows and murmured orders to them.

The young men snapped to attention and served the first course: crab bisque.

Ash sat at the head of the table and then opened his napkin, laying it across his hips. A strange heat seemed to emanate from his gaze as he eyed the decanter of Madeira. Then a slight smile curved his lips as Ash lifted the spoon to his mouth.

What was he thinking about? She couldn't hazard to guess.

Chastity was fascinated by his elegant manners. Even quietly slurping his bisque aroused her.

I am becoming quite hopelessly besotted with him.

By the time the mulled wine sorbet arrived, Ash had engaged Hannah in a lively conversation about horses. Hannah had always loved them but had no opportunity to interact with the animals as the family had always lived in the city with no means to own a carriage and horses.

"And what about you, Jon? Do you also love horses?" Ash asked politely.

Jon looked away, a slight sneer forming at the corner of his mouth. Chastity wished she could reach under the table and give her brother a swift kick to his shin. She tried to do that very thing. Alas, the table proved too wide.

She glared at him, daring him to respond.

"Jon? I am speaking to you." Ash did not sound cross. His tone was friendly but firm.

"I suppose so," Jon grumbled in response, shrugging. "I've never ridden one nor had lessons," he paused. "My lord."

Chastity exhaled in relief. Not entirely respectful, but a satisfactory reply. Jon will need to be set straight again about his lack of manners.

The footmen carried away the empty dishes and served beef wellington with shallot pudding, roasted zucchini, and carrots. The feast was fit for a king. Never had she eaten such an elegant meal.

"I keep a fine stable at Wenlock," Ash professed. "My country seat is about an hour's train ride from here, not far from Worthing. If you like, we can plan a trip to Wenlock Manor. Jon, you and Hannah can satisfy your curiosity for horses. The head groom and his lads would happily give you both lessons."

Hannah broke into excited chatter, and Jon appeared shocked, as if he could not believe the offer. A suspicious look darkened his eyes. Chastity recognized it well enough after what they all had been through. She could not blame Jon for his reaction.

The trust had been beaten out of them these past years.

If she were honest, she did not have complete faith in Ash, despite his generosity and compassion. The baron had done nothing to rally such mistrust, but she could not help it.

A small degree of caution would not go amiss. Life and circumstance had made her cynical and suspicious. For her brother's and sister's sake, she must remain vigilant.

Chastity cut into the beef and pastry dish and took a delicate bite. Glancing at Ash, he gave her a playful wink. The man was far too sensual for his own good. A slight flutter of his eyelid, and she reacted on cue. Her insides tumbled with desire.

Clearing her throat, Chastity returned her attention to the delicious food before her.

"If you have any meal suggestions, a certain pastry or cake you wish, please let Grimes know. He will arrange it with the housekeeper and cook," Ash said.

"Trifle!" Hannah called out. Then she placed her hand across her mouth. "Sorry, my lord."

Ash chuckled. "No apology needed. Hannah, you will have a trifle for the luncheon as soon as possible. Chastity? There must be something you have wished for regarding food."

"My father brought me a Napoléon from a French pastry shop for a birthday treat. It is puff pastry with whipped cream and icing with chocolate stripes."

"I've had them. I will see it done. Jon?"

"Nothing. I want nothing."

The short interest he had shown over the discussion of horses was gone. The moody look had returned.

"Jon," Chastity admonished.

"Cake, then. A sponge cake with blackberry jam filling and buttercream on top. I also wish we were back home and my parents were still alive. Can you make that happen, my lord? Is that in your power, then, to take away all the horrific memories? Because if it is, I will be polite, bow, and scrape as much as you like." The words tumbled out of Jon in a rush, his voice cracking on the last few words.

Chastity's heart squeezed at the sound of her brother's anguish.

"I am sorry, but I cannot undo all that has transpired. If I could, I would take away the hurt and pain you have all endured," Ash replied, his voice soft and soothing. "I want you to know this, both you and Hannah. I will not hold your sister to the agreement. I offer my assistance to you all. Stay here as my guests. Recover from your ordeal. Will you think about it? Jon?"

"Yes, I will."

"Good man."

The rest of the meal passed pleasantly. After a dessert of peach tarts and apple crumble, the governess arrived to escort the children to their rooms. Ash dismissed the footmen.

Chastity stood, but Ash laid a hand gently on her arm to halt her. Her skin immediately ignited from his touch.

"Could remain a moment, Chastity, if you please?"

Chapter 13

ASH REMOVED HIS HAND and refilled their wine glasses. "Why did you suggest this arrangement? Indulge me." His voice was low, the tone questioning.

What could she say?

Chastity sipped her wine, crafting her reply. "I am unsure how to answer that query without sounding mercenary."

"So, the only reason you made the suggestion was the money and protection that I could offer. What a decided blow to my masculine ego."

"What do you wish me to say, Ash? That your kiss at the inn ignited a passion I did not know existed? That I find you handsome beyond words?"

He gave her a warm smile. "That is as good a place as any to start."

"Well, that is the truth. Beyond all that, it is how you have opened your home in welcome. The courtesy and patience you have shown Jon and Hannah. The generosity in buying the clothes, the governess, the offer of riding lessons and desserts, what man does that? A gentleman."

Chastity exhaled and laid her hand on top of his. "Yes, it was either go with you or starve. But this past week, I've developed—am developing—feelings for you. I suppose a mistress should not be admitting to such emotional frailties, but there it is."

"This is what I have been longing to hear. I appreciate your honesty," Ash murmured silkily.

"I am not a proper mistress any more than I was a true prossie. I'm in your employ; you deserve my gratitude and respect. Also, I should not have spoken to you the way I did this afternoon. I'm sorry."

Ash laced his fingers through hers and clasped her hand tight. "No need for forgiveness. I wish for you to speak your mind when we are alone together. And please cease with this employer-employee paradigm. I don't want that to be the sum total of our relationship. And I do want one." He kissed her hand and released it. "Do not refer to yourself as a mistress again. Please."

"Very well, I won't. You puzzle me exceedingly. But then, I cannot fathom my actions and reactions, so why would I be capable of discerning yours?" Chastity whispered.

Ash held up his wine glass. "Cheers. I have been experiencing the same. We are a pair."

"So, we're to suspend physical activities?"

"For the time being. I wish for you to come to my bed of your own accord because you want to. Not because you suggested being my mistress, and I had a contract drawn up for you to sign."

"I did sign it, and of my own free will."

"I know. I'll toss the thing in the fire tonight if you wish."

"No, at least not yet. I can't explain it."

"I understand it offers you a sense of security. Whenever you say."

"Yes, I think you have hit on it. A sense of security. Oh, this situation is muddled, isn't it?" she sighed.

"We will figure it out at some point, I am certain. That's why I invited you all to dinner. I also want to know your brother and sister better. As I said, we all should not be strangers."

Ash paused and sipped his wine thoughtfully. "There must be more between the two of us than sex. I yearn for there to be. Do you feel the same?"

"I need time to ponder all this."

"Then you shall have it. I can be patient."

"As I said, you *are* a gentleman."

Ash scoffed. "I am not a gentleman, Chastity. Not like my father. Why do you suppose I was in the vicinity of Shag Alley? It can be argued that I'm a young man unhindered and free to do as I please. Believe me when I tell you—I have."

She arched an eyebrow. "Are you telling me that you are a rake after all?"

A husky chuckle rumbled from his chest. "No more than you were a prostitute. I played at it. My heart was not in it. Well, at least this past year. I was part of the group for the long-standing friendships with some members more than anything else. You are the first I have admitted this to."

Ash stroked the top of her hand with his thumb, and the flame rolling through her increased. "As I told you, I've never had a mistress. I am no doubt making a hash of this entire situation. In fact, I know I have. I am aware I've acted strangely. I cannot adequately explain it. I will confess the kiss at the inn was also a revelation to me."

Ash released her hand and refilled their wine glasses.

"I've not experienced such intense and confusing emotions before. And therefore, I had no clue how to respond. Stupidly, I believed that I should stay distant in our dealings. My sincere apologies."

Ash's beautiful eyes radiated tender warmth and also a burning desire. His heartfelt confession touched her in an uncharted area of her heart. Her insides fluttered madly at his words.

At this moment, she fell a little in love with Asher Colborne.

"I accept your apology, and I am glad we are being honest," Chastity replied earnestly.

"As am I. Let us continue to keep communication open. I abhor misunderstandings that are not addressed in a timely manner."

"Yes, I agree. Since we are communicating, tell me about yourself and your life," Chastity said.

"Me? As you had stated so succinctly, I wanted for nothing. My parents loved each other, a rarity amongst the aristocrats. Which meant I was brought up in a warm and happy home. Unlike most of my friends."

"You have no siblings?"

"No. Well, I almost did. My mother was told she could not have more children, so imagine my parents' surprise when they were told she was expecting. I was nineteen at the time, away at university. Completely oblivious to what crisis had occurred at home. My father came to see me after my mother died and brought me home for the funeral. It was a horrible blow to us. My mother was the heart of our family."

"Oh, Ash. I am sorry."

"I didn't learn what had happened until a couple of years later. It was a tubal pregnancy. Which meant the baby grew outside the womb. Her insides ruptured."

Chastity gasped, her hand flying to her mouth in shock. "Oh, no!"

"My father never recovered. He lived another six years but was a shell of his former self. I believe he died of a broken heart. My heart broke as well. Not only for my dear mother but for the agonizing grief my father lived with. I swore I would never love like that. It was a declaration most of my friends shared, in one way or another—and for one reason or another."

"The ones in your rake group?" she asked softly.

"Yes. Some of us that grew up together. We shared sorrows and joys and became brothers, as none of us had siblings. We formed a protective ring, keeping emotions at bay and allowing no one to hurt us, as a few of my friends have had terrible family lives. And we indulged in certain vices as carefree, arrogant peers often do."

"I am glad you have good friends to turn to."

Ash arched an eyebrow. "And you did not?"

"Oh, I had a few close friends. I even toyed with going to them for help when we ran away. But it would be the first place Barrington would look. Or so I thought."

"When things are more settled, you should contact your friends." Ash took her hand and kissed it. Then he laced his fingers through hers.

"I will. If things ever settle," Chastity sighed.

"They will. I am hopeful. And I believe we will be able to come to terms with those intense emotions we spoke of." Ash gave her a warm smile, causing her insides to flutter.

Intense emotions.

Chastity could understand what he meant, for she felt the same. It was best to take this one day at a time, but she vowed to open her heart more, to learn to trust. To know Ash better.

For once, the future had promise.

"It is a beautiful night and unseasonably warm," Ash continued. "Why don't we take a stroll along the street? There is a park area near here where we can watch the sunset. It is why I suggested dinner be served early."

"I would like that."

"I will have William fetch your wrap."

After they affixed their cloaks and gloves, Ash placed his hat on his head, and once they stepped onto the walkway, he offered his arm. Chastity pulled the hood up of her wool cloak as it might obscure her face. The affluent and handsome Baron Wenlock promenading along his street with a strange woman may excite comment.

They hadn't traversed too far when they passed another young couple, and Ash politely inclined his head.

"This wasn't a good idea," Chastity murmured. "There may be gossip. I do not wish to cause you any unwanted attention from society."

Ash patted her hand. "A baron hardly excites comment from the upper echelons of society. Besides, there is hardly anyone on the street."

Chastity blew out a breath of relief. After nearly three years of looking about for any impending danger—and it was everywhere regardless of where they lived while on the run—it wasn't easy to relax. But Chastity decided to start tonight by enjoying the sights and sounds around her. The exterior of Ash's town house was impressive, with all the white stucco, columns, and light sandstone bricks. And it had a terrace overlooking the street. Chastity had no idea. But then, she had arrived here late at night, so distraught she never took in her surroundings.

"What a lovely neighborhood. I never asked, what street is this?"

"Eaton Place, Belgravia. My father liked the quiet, which is why he picked it after my mother passed. It's become home to me. I do not have a separate staff. They travel with me from Wenlock Manor. I haven't been back there in many months."

"Do you prefer city life?"

"No. I like both; equally, both have their good points. It is difficult to have French pastries delivered at a moment's notice at the manor."

Chastity chuckled.

"But then, with too much time spent in London, I long for the fresh air, going for long rides on my horse, being involved in the running of the estate."

Ash led her to a park bench and assisted her in taking her seat. He sat next to her, closer than what should be proper. His leg pressed against hers. The contact was searing, even through layers of clothes. They sat together for the longest time, watching the sun slowly disappear behind the buildings.

Chastity watched a man and a young boy travel along the street, using a ladder to light the gas lamps. The illumination cast a soft glow over the area.

"The man and his son, as this job is often passed along within families, will return at dawn to extinguish the light. It is a noble profession with great responsibility and trust."

The man waved in their direction. "Good evening, my lord."

"Good evening to you, Mr. Blackstock."

The lamplighter returned to his duties, with the young boy dutifully holding the ladder, then passing the wick trimmer to Mr. Blackstock.

"You know his name?"

"I do. My father always said to treat those around you respectfully, especially those who labor in honest occupations."

"I wish more of your class thought the same way."

Ash took her gloved hand and laced his fingers through his. Taking part of her cloak, he draped it over their joined hands. "There. No one to see. Try and remove all worries from your mind. Enjoy the sunset. The pale gold shade is due to the coal smoke. Out in the country, that shade would be a vibrant orange. As I said, both have their good points." Ash turned slightly in his seat and nuzzled her neck. "But being with you moves my heart more than a beautiful sunset. You outshine it all."

Chastity's heart sped up at his softly spoken words. Without thinking, Chastity gently grazed his cheek. In looking up, she saw Mr. Blackstock smiling at them. He touched his forelock and moved on to the next gas lamp.

Sighing, she laid her head on Ash's shoulder, and still holding hands, they stayed on the bench until darkness covered them.

What a wonderful evening. One to hold close to her heart and in her memories. No matter what the future would bring, she'd remember this night.

Chapter 14

SIX DAYS HAD PASSED, and the atmosphere at Eaton Place had lightened considerably. They had shared more meals. Ash made daily inquiries about her sibling's studies. But Ash also gave her and her siblings time to relax and heal, just as he said.

Chastity was doing that very thing, curled up by the small fireplace in her bedroom, a quilt across her lap, reading a book. And for once, she could concentrate on the words and immerse herself in the story. It was amazing that she felt better already.

Hannah burst into the room. "Chastity, come to the upstairs sitting room at once! There is a surprise for us all!"

How gratifying to see girlish enthusiasm back in Hannah's life. Chastity had feared it was gone for good.

"Oh, do come," Hannah cried, pulling on her arm.

"All right, my dear."

Placing her book upside down on the table, Chastity tossed aside the quilt and followed Hannah upstairs. When they entered the sitting room, Chastity audibly gasped at the sight.

Afternoon tea was laid out with china cups, saucers, and silver tea service. Taking Chastity's hand, Hannah skipped around the table, pointing.

"Look, a trifle! And the blackberry sponge and your puff pastries. Isn't the baron fabulous?"

Jon took a seat at the table. "Maybe he's not so bad," he grumbled.

Chastity immediately poured the tea and served the desserts.

Jon devoured his cake in no time at all. Smiling, with a bit of blackberry jam adhered to the corner of his lips, he held out his empty plate. "Another slice, if you please."

Laughing, Chastity gave them all second helpings.

"We must not take advantage of his lordship's generosity," Chastity declared as her fork sliced through the delicate puff pastry of her Napoléon.

"Did he mean what he said? About you not being his kept woman anymore?" Jon asked.

Chastity nearly choked on the whipped cream.

"Jon. That is not an appropriate discussion, especially with your sister present. We are here as his lordship's guests only. Do you take my meaning? But we cannot stay here indefinitely. After a few weeks of recovery, we have to make other arrangements. Other—plans."

Hannah's eyes grew wide. "We have to leave?"

"Not right away, Hannah," a deep voice interjected.

They all turned to find Ash leaning against the door frame. He held up a teacup and saucer.

"I brought my own cup. May I join you? I must say, that blackberry sponge called to me all the way from my study."

Hannah giggled, then took a mouthful of trifle.

"Yes, please join us," Chastity said warmly, reacting to his potent presence. All he had to do was walk into a room to set her heart racing.

He handed her the cup and saucer, and Chastity poured him tea.

Taking his cup, Ash sat opposite the children. "All your favorites as you requested. My cook, Mrs. Ironbridge, made the trifle and the sponge cake, but I had the pastries delivered from a nearby shop. How is everything?"

"Absolutely wonderful," Chastity said, her voice low. Her heart swelled with emotions she could not name. "Hannah, Jon?"

"Thank you, my lord," they said in near-perfect unison.

"You are most welcome. If you come up with other suggestions, I will see that we have afternoon tea here next week at the same time. I, for one, am going to ask for raspberry tarts," Ash declared.

Jon laid his fork across the edge of his plate. "Thank you, my lord, for everything. I am sorry I acted the way I have. I will try to use the manners my parents taught me."

"Jon, I have no idea what you have all endured. How can I? But you have every right to be suspicious and protective of your sisters. I admire that. Trust has to be earned."

Jon nodded, his cheeks slightly flushed.

Chastity's heart warmed at Jon's declaration. It was a good start.

After second—and in Jon's case—third helpings, the governess arrived to escort the children to the schoolroom. Ash insisted that Miss Tallen take a choice of dessert. At first, she refused, but with coaxing, the governess chose the Napoléon.

Chastity and Ash were left alone.

"More tea?" she asked.

"Yes. And further conversation."

"I enjoyed our conversation last night," Chastity stated as she poured him another cup. "And our walk in the park."

"As did I. You looked quite beautiful in your fur-lined hooded cloak."

"Thank you. I love it."

"Do you mind if I ask some rather probing questions?"

"Depends on the subject," Chastity replied as she sipped her tea.

"Please tell me about your life over the past few years. I truly wish to know. And it is not for my amusement."

"I know that," she replied gently. "Where to begin? Perhaps at the end, when you came upon us. The situation was quite dismal. I realize that now. Hannah had been ill so often in the past years; her cough worsened each time."

"I noticed a lingering cough. I will call a doctor. I should have done so when you all first arrived. It is unhealthy for all of you to be locked up like this. Even though the weather is growing colder by the day, we should take a ride in the carriage," Ash said. "And I would like to take you all to dinner. I know of a place with a private dining room. We can enjoy a meal in complete solitude."

"Thank you, about the doctor. And a ride and dinner would be enjoyable."

"The place is called Scott's Oyster and Supper Rooms. Do you all like seafood? That is their specialty. Although, I can have them prepare just about anything, especially for the children."

"I will ask them."

"Christmas is less than three weeks away. Will you all spend it here with me?"

"Oh," Chastity sighed. "We haven't had a proper Christmas since my father died. Sir Nigel would not allow us to put up a tree."

"Miserable man. Then we will be certain to have one. Will you stay?"

"Yes. But then what?"

"I'll come up with something, never you fear."

Without thinking, Chastity clasped his hand tight. "I do believe you will come up with a plan. Thank you again."

"You are most welcome. Tell me about the night you fled," he asked softly. "I swear that this request is not for my twisted enjoyment. I truly wish to know. Tell me what you endured so I can understand the plight of those with nowhere to turn. I plan to take up many causes in Parliament, and the more I know, the better prepared I will be to make a persuasive argument."

Chastity looked into his eyes. There was no mockery there, only empathy. Talking about it may help to banish the memories. It was worth a try.

"After I rendered Sir Nigel unconscious, we changed clothes. We had to get out of there before he awoke. If I had been thinking more clearly, I could have snatched items worth bartering or food from the kitchen. But I had no other thought but to flee. I did stuff things from my room in a small carpetbag. A blanket, my comb, brush, matches, and a book, if you can imagine. I should have checked Barrington's pockets as he undoubtedly had a few pounds on him."

Chastity exhaled. "What did I know of surviving on the streets? Thank goodness we brought our coats and boots. That first night, we slept behind my father's law office building—or where his office used to be. After that, we headed to the East End, where the cheapest lodgings could be found. I sold the silver brush for a couple of pounds. With it, I bought bread and cheese for our travels and the occasional bed at a dosshouse."

"My God. It is a wonder you were not attacked."

"We very nearly were and more than once. I soon learned that our clean coats drew unwanted attention. I sold them and bought us second-hand ones. As the days passed, we blended in with the 'great unwashed' as Sir Nigel called those living in the East End. I couldn't allow him to track us down. I eventually came to the shocking realization that he probably never initiated a search. Though relieved, I remained vigilant."

"How did you live for the following months and years?" Ash asked, clearly riveted by her narrative.

Chastity could also see the concern on Ash's face, which gave her the courage to continue. Even speaking of this sparked twisting anxiety deep inside her, so much for trying to banish the memories. But she would continue on, regardless.

"We managed to earn a shilling here and there. I sold the book and pieces of clothing, and I had a gold cross with a small diamond around my neck, a birthday gift from my parents. It broke my heart to sell it. But it kept us fed and housed for several weeks."

Her voice shook, but she continued. "We all did what tasks we could to earn a crust. Sold every possession. Have you ever gone to bed hungry?"

Ash shook his head. "No. Never."

"The cramps become so severe even tears will not come. Did Jon resort to thievery? Yes, I believe so. I didn't ask where he happened to find a wayward apple or chunk of cheese or piece of beef. We did what we had to do to survive. For a time, I scrubbed floors in a pub. You haven't lived until you mopped up vomit, tobacco spittle, spilled beer, and worse. The sticky substance men expel from—"

"Enough. My poor, dear."

"No. I must continue while I dare to speak of it. When things became hopeless and we had no other recourse, I went to Shag Alley. I lost my virtue to a drunken, smelly man who was rough and foul. Thankfully, the act ended quickly enough. No woman should endure such humiliation or lose so much to live. To eat. But for Jon and Hannah, I would have done much more."

"You said it happened twice?" he asked gently.

"Yes, as I said, the second time, I am not sure he even stuck it in me. The landlord—"

"Loathsome fellow."

"Yes, we were behind in the rent. The landlord had offered that I work it off by servicing *him*. I had put it off as long as I could. You literally saved me from further humiliation."

Ash growled. "I am sorry I paid that bastard the back rent. I wish I had known this sooner. A sound beating is what he deserves."

"I agree. But I'm glad we are well clear of that landlord. I am forever saying thank you, but I say it once again. For settling the rent."

"That place wasn't fit for man or beast," Ash said. "I am still angry about the landlord. Perhaps I *will* pay him a visit and give him a taste of his own medicine."

Chastity clutched his arm. "No, please. Let us forget that man even exists. However, those squalid places *do* exist. Entire families are in one or two rooms. It's shameful in such a wealthy country."

"I agree. My privilege is shameful. I looked away; I did not help."

"But you can foster change—in Parliament."

"Yes. I can. And I will."

She smiled. "I am glad to hear it."

"I am serious. More must be done. A few in the House of Lords want to effect change in society for those less fortunate. I will be sure to seek them out."

Chastity sat back in her chair and took another sip of tea. "Good. There is no security in most situations. Anyone not wealthy could find themselves on the street due to unforeseen circumstances. It is not right. I am gratified to hear some peers care enough to look into the matter."

She sighed wistfully. "Even though we are removed from that horrible place and situation, I still worry about Jon and Hannah. Though for Jon, it is not of a physical nature. I think something happened. He alluded to it the first morning we arrived here. It chilled my blood. He said, 'It's my fault we had to leave! If I had only done what he wanted.' He said never to ask him. He was speaking of Sir Nigel. I know it."

Ash stood and gathered her into his arms. "May I say how unselfish it is for you to be more concerned about your siblings than yourself? Everything you have done was to keep them safe. I admire that. You are a courageous woman, Chastity Armitage."

"My poor brother and sister."

"Leave it with me. No more worries today."

Chastity gazed up at him, and something seized in her chest. Ash looked at her with a combination of sympathy and longing. She stroked his chin, her touch reigniting the flame within.

"I want you to do something for me, Chastity."

"Yes?"

"It won't be easy."

He kissed her. A gentle, soul-stirring kiss that sent heat clear to her toes. He dove deep, then slowly ended it by nibbling her lower lip.

"Forget the horrors. Remember...me."

Yes. Forgetting the horrors would not be simple at all. But Chastity would remember Ash and that wonderful kiss. And his kindness and generosity.

Come to his bed of her own volition and not as his mistress. That may be happening sooner than she imagined.

For she was more than besotted.

Chastity was falling in love with Asher Colborne.

Chapter 15

AFTER A CARRIAGE RIDE in Hyde Park, Asher escorted the Armitages through a private entrance in the rear of the building at Scott's Oyster and Supper Rooms on Coventry Street.

"The outside of the building is stunning," Chastity enthused. "The ironwork and the sculptures of shells and fishes. Oh, Ash. This looks expensive. I should not have said that."

"You can say whatever you like. And it is expensive, and you all deserve a treat," Asher smiled warmly.

The head waiter led them to one of the private dining rooms. The room was well-appointed, with golden and green accents, a crystal chandelier, and silk wallpaper. Asher pulled the chair for Chastity to sit in, then did the same for Hannah.

"As per your instructions, my lord, all is ready," the waiter said as he poured ice water into crystal goblets. "Shall I start with the lime sorbet and beetroot salad?"

"Yes. In about ten minutes."

The waiter bowed and quit the room.

"I hope you don't mind, but I ordered for all of us in advance when I booked this room. After the first few courses, Roberto, the head waiter on this floor—whose real name is Bobby Hinkenbottom—"

The Armitages laughed.

"Roberto will bring in platters of food, mostly seafood, as that is their specialty. But also beefsteak and roasted chicken, so there should be plenty to choose from. Chastity tells me you both enjoy shrimp."

"Yes, my lord. We only had it a few times, but we all like it." Jon replied. At least the lad was acting less surly when conversing. It was a start in the right direction.

"I asked Roberto about the history. This place started as an oyster warehouse by a fishmonger named John Scott. It is now one of the premier seafood restaurants in London. It was refurbished a few years ago with Bath stone in a French renaissance style."

"It is lovely," Chastity smiled. "Thank you for bringing us here. What else did Roberto tell you?"

"There are numerous floors, with a wine and coffee bar, a lobster boiling room, an oyster bar, and a grilling room. Plus two floors of dining rooms, from the large main one to smaller private ones such as this. I have been here a few times before. I am not fond of oysters, but I enjoy their seared scallops. Of which I ordered. Ah. Here are the first courses."

Asher wanted to keep the conversation light tonight, with no mention of Barrington or their situation or their future. If any family deserved to be pampered, it was Chastity and her siblings.

Everyone oohed when Roberto and another waiter set the platters of food in the middle of the large round table. Grilled Dover sole, seared scallops, smoked halibut, Dublin shrimp, both potted and grilled, along with the beef and chicken. Next came the vegetables.

"Thank you, Roberto. We can serve ourselves." The servers departed.

"This is not on the menu," Asher pointed. "But the chef made them special for tonight. Chipped potatoes. Or, as some refer to it—chips. They are deep fried in oil."

"We've had them once," Jon whispered. "I stole them from a vendor in Bethnal Green."

Silence descended over the table.

"And that warm food fed you and your sisters," Asher stated. "Do not dwell on it, Jon. Instead, enjoy the meal before you, and know those days are behind you. Never to return." Asher took the silver tongs and served the chips to them. "Eat them while they are hot. And speaking of chips, a new restaurant opened two years ago, making fish and chips no longer just for street vendors. The place has tablecloths, fancy cutlery, and china, and the fish and chips, bread and butter, and tea can be had for nine pence."

"Can we go there, too?" Hannah asked.

Asher gave Hannah a sincere smile. "Of course, we can. Just before Christmas. That way, we can see the lights and decorations on the various city streets."

Jon remained quiet for a time but eventually rejoined the conversation.

"Will we visit your country estate to see the horses soon?" Hannah asked.

"Hannah!" Chastity admonished.

"I do not mind, Chastity. Hannah, we can discuss that after Christmas, I promise. Jon, would you like to go with the footmen to obtain a proper tree for the holiday? And we will need pine boughs as well. You will be gone for the afternoon. Cedric and Nigel are good lads, not much older than you. They will be good company. Sometime later next week, I imagine."

Jon nodded. "Thank you, my lord."

After a dessert of treacle sponge cake and Bakewell pudding, they all rose to depart.

Chastity looked at him questioningly at the waiters carrying hampers toward the rear exit.

"My father taught me never to waste a crumb of food. What is left, I am giving to the servants, or we can have some of this for luncheon tomorrow. If there is any remaining after that, one of the footmen will take it to a nearby soup kitchen."

"I like that. I wish more did the same," Chastity replied as he laid her cloak over her shoulders.

And that could be something he could arrange for Chastity to be involved in if she wished it. Asher would think on it some more. All in all, it was a wonderful evening.

THREE DAYS LATER, ASHER entered his study and found Jon Armitage examining the many books that filled the wall-to-wall bookcases. Once he spotted Asher, Jon lowered his head and moved toward the door. The lad was still acting apprehensive.

"Wait. I want to speak to you for a moment, Jon."

Asher closed the door and motioned for the boy to sit in one of the leather chairs by the window.

"Anytime you wish to borrow a book to read, please do so. I did say that you could."

Jon's head snapped up. "You don't mind, my lord?"

Jon did not believe me the other day?

Asher sat in the opposite chair and crossed his legs.

"Not at all. Your governess tells me that you continue to excel at your lessons. Do you have any inkling of what you would like to do with any profession or trade?"

Jon's thick brows knitted as if deep in thought. "I wondered, my lord, if it were possible to follow my late father into law. A barrister, perhaps. Or a solicitor as he was. Though I would make sure that I never make bad investments."

Chastity had mentioned that their father brought them into abject poverty with wrong-headed investment schemes. It made an impression on Jon.

"A bold ambition and a worthy one. Why not, indeed? Would you be averse to going away to school in about six months? Perhaps to Westminster or Charterhouse. Then, when you're old enough, you could apprentice to be a solicitor, or we could work to have you called to the bar should you wish to be a barrister. I would sponsor you as I have connections with various law firms who would gladly foster your ambitions."

Jon's eyes widened. "You would do this—for me? I'm nobody to you. Why? Because of my sister?"

Why indeed? Asher was proposing a long-term commitment. He need not concern himself with the Armitages if he and Chastity went their separate ways.

But that is not what Asher wanted. And it was not the man he desired to be. He wished to help the boy. Having the intelligent lad flounder in a lower existence would be an abject waste.

The chance that he could undermine Sir Nigel appealed, even though the man still held custody of the children. At least, Asher assumed it. Those were details that had to be worked out. Also, what Chastity had told him in confidence about Jon picked at his heart.

"I'll not lie to you. Part of it has to do with your sister. I saw her close to three years ago at a ball. I was smitten at first sight. When I found out about her guardian, and my father and I paid a visit to gain a formal introduction, Sir Nigel informed us that you all had permanently relocated to Northern Scotland."

Asher allowed the knowledge to sink in.

Jon clenched his fists, his cheeks flushed, but he said nothing. Chastity must not have informed him of this information.

"Lad, you are not a nobody. You warrant a chance at a decent life. Your mother and sister sacrificed for you and Hannah to have all you deserve. Do not let their oblation be in vain."

"I won't, my lord. Thank you. How did you come across Chastity again?"

"After a night of cards with friends, I saw your sister standing under a streetlamp. She would only come with me if I guaranteed certain provisions and agreements, especially for you and Hannah. The circumstances of our arrangement are private. How could I not offer to help, especially after seeing your living conditions? You know you all would have perished? That your situation was desperate?"

"Yes. I know it," Jon whispered. "I did what I could, but it was never enough."

"I understand. I care very much for your sister. And for you and Hannah. You are safe here; you can trust me. I understand it will take time to adjust to your new situation. And to have confidence in me. As I said at dinner, you are here as my guests. Your sister does not have to be my—employee for you all to stay. You are old enough to comprehend my meaning."

"Yes, my lord."

"This is not charity. I am investing in your career. Once you reach the age of majority, I expect you to care for your sisters and see to their well-being," Asher continued. "At some point, I will have to speak to your stepfather regarding your custody."

The look of horror that passed across Jon's features shook him. The boy paled to the shade of chalk. Something *had* occurred after all. He had only mentioned the man to see Jon's reaction. Asher wished now that he hadn't.

"What happened, Jon?" he asked gently.

"I can't speak of it."

"It would stay between us, two men sharing confidences. You have my word as a gentleman and a lord," Asher stated firmly.

Jon exhaled shakily. "You can't tell Chastity. Ever. Promise me, my lord."

"I promise. This is what I spoke about. This is how we build trust."

Jon nodded, rubbing his hands together, clearly showing his anxiety. "Soon after our mother's funeral, Sir Nigel tried to get me alone more than once. He told me if I did certain things—and he described them in detail—he would see Chastity properly married. If I did not, he would throw us out into the streets. He kissed me on the lips and stuck his tongue down my throat on three different occasions."

Jon shuddered. "Two nights later, he pulled me into the pantry. He wanted me to—touch him." A wretched sob caught in Jon's throat. "I didn't do it, but I knew he would not stop at a grope in a dark cupboard. That he wouldn't leave me alone. What if he turned his foul eyes toward Hannah?"

If there were a special place in hell for men who took advantage of innocent children, he would see to it that fucking reprobate made it there in a timely manner. Banking his rage, he waited for Jon to collect himself. After exhaling, the lad continued.

"Sir Nigel said he would come to me soon and—I never told Chastity any details, but she must have sensed something, for she started sleeping in my room either by the door or on the settee. The night he tried to climb into my bed, Chastity knocked him insensible with the warming pan."

His admiration for Chastity raised several notches. Good for her. God, she was magnificent. This steeled his resolve to see no further harm came to Chastity and her siblings. And to think all this occurred after seeing her at the ball.

"That is the night you all ran, correct?"

Jon nodded and then sniffled.

"He did not try anything else with you?"

Jon shook his head vigorously.

Asher stood and laid a hand on Jon's shoulder. "Listen to me. You have done nothing wrong. Do not blame yourself for a situation you had no control over. There was no one to turn to, nowhere to go. Barrington, and others like him, are pustules of a decent society. I will do all in my power to see that man never bothers you again," Asher declared, his voice determined.

And by God, he meant every word.

Jon rose from the chair and encircled his arms around Asher's waist, sniffing noisily into his waistcoat. The poor lad was starved for affection. He patted the top of Jon's head in comfort. After what the boy went through with Sir Nigel, Jon embracing him showed that trust and respect had taken root between them. Jon's show of emotion genuinely touched Asher.

"There, the worst is over. You have a home here. All is not lost."

"T-t-thank you for the clothes, my lord. And e-e-everything," Jon stammered. "But for listening, most of all."

Asher's heart ached not only for Jon but for Chastity and Hannah.

How many others lived in such terrible conditions?

It was too horrifying to contemplate.

Though he couldn't save everyone, he would start with the Armitage family. Then, as Asher promised Chastity, work in Parliament to further the cause of women and children.

Christian had mentioned he held numerous conversations with Aidan Wollstonecraft, the Earl of Carnstone, a champion for the poor for decades. Harrison Hornsby, the Duke of Gransford, also worked diligently to try and bring affordable healthcare to the poor.

Asher would ask to join the various efforts.

Yes, a solid first step.

Jon stepped back and wiped his eyes. Looking up at Asher, he held out his hand. "Thank you, my lord. I will do my utmost to be worthy of the chance you are giving me. I will look after my sisters."

Asher took Jon's hand and shook it. "Well said. You *are* the man of the family."

"Forgive me for interrupting, my lord," Grimes said. "You have received a note from the Duke of Allenby requiring an immediate response, the messenger said."

"Jon, continue to look over the books. I will take this in the parlor."

Once in the parlor, Grimes handed him the sealed note. Asher tore it open.

ASHER,

If you are available, come at once to Cleveland Street. We will be here all afternoon. Althea has some information regarding the case.
Christian

WELL, THAT WAS QUICK. It had only been a week.

Asher stuffed the note in the side pocket of his jacket.

"Have the carriage brought around. I will meet the duke at The Galway Agency on Cleveland Street."

"At once, my lord."

In a matter of minutes, Asher headed toward Cleveland Street. The conversation with Jon played in his head. Jon had been assaulted, but the violation had not reached its horrible conclusion.

Regardless, the damage had been done; how could it not be?

Rest and heal.

All the Armitages needed it.

And Asher was glad he had suspended physical relations between him and Chastity.

Shown into the parlor by the Galway housekeeper, Mrs. Bartle, Asher found Althea, Eleanora, and Christian sitting and drinking tea.

"Just in time, have a seat. Beefsteak sandwiches, your favorite," Christian said.

Settling in, Asher filled his plate. "And they are also your favorite. I'm impressed, Althea. Information already?"

"Well, with assistance from Eleanora and Christian. There is still more to discover; I've no doubt. Christian? You go first."

"You are part of the firm, then, Your Grace?" Asher teased.

"Of course, I assist when I can. I assumed it would be me if anyone could pry gossip out of unsuspecting peers. I'm a duke, after all," Christian winked mischievously. "Barrington was made a knight in service to the crown. He wasn't a spy in the strictest sense of the word. During the Third Burma War, around eighteen eighty-five, he was made captain because of important information he had provided that aided in thwarting a small uprising."

"Please don't tell me this degenerate is a war hero," Asher groaned. "Or I may be physically ill here on the carpet."

"No. Not a hero in the strictest sense. Barrington never saw combat. He relayed information he had overheard in a drinking establishment in Rangoon. Or so the story goes," Christian replied.

"Well, if he saved British lives, that explains the knighthood. Damn his eyes," Asher grunted.

"It may be the only decent thing the man has done in his life," Althea interjected as she turned the pages of her notebook. "I could not find anyone who spoke well of him. Words like 'haughty, arrogant, cruel' were among the few adjectives used. One acquaintance even questioned how his wife died, the mother of the Armitages."

Asher cocked an eyebrow.

"That's where I come in, "Eleanora remarked. "Archie did some digging, found the doctor, and examined his records. Amelia Barrington died of cancer of the stomach. She had been ill for several months."

Archie was a young lad of fourteen. He had lived on the streets for two years and had done odd jobs for the Galway sisters. Christian now sponsored the lad, giving him room, board, and education, while Archie worked part-time for The Galway Agency, honing his already impressive investigative skills.

"Looked at his records? How was that achieved?" Asher asked, bemusement in his tone.

"In the usual way, I imagine. We don't question Archie's methods, not when they glean results. I assume the Armitage children were never told what their mother died of?" Christian asked.

"No. Not as far as I know. Just that it was sudden."

Althea held up her battered notebook. "I found the barrister Sir Nigel used when he relayed to the children that he had custody of them."

Asher was impressed at the thoroughness of the investigation so far.

"He has a dingy office in the East End," Althea continued. "Mr. Uriah Bruce of Whitechapel. Why would a knight deal with such a shady character? They've been acquainted since they were boys. Not friends as they hardly travel in the same social circles, but someone who would lie for him—for a price."

"Well done, all of you. Allow me to relay my conversation with my solicitor, Mr. Peebles."

Asher mentioned the various laws, the ins and outs of guardianship, and the possibility of a will; one Amelia made while still a widow.

"But there were only three weeks from her husband's death until she married Barrington. And where would she get the money for such an expense as making a will?" Eleanora asked.

Asher's heart dropped to his toes. He had never considered that. "Then, if there is a will, it was made after her second marriage, and Barrington knew the contents. He still could be lying. Chastity was never shown any documents."

"Then that will be our next line of inquiry," Althea said. "I will contact your Mr. Peebles immediately."

Asher raised his teacup. "To the Galway Agency. I am quite dazzled by your collective skills."

There may be a happy conclusion after all.

Asher wanted nothing more than for Chastity and her siblings to be safe and secure.

Chapter 16

ANOTHER WEEK HAD PASSED, and Chastity had settled into a quiet routine of sleep, reading, and eating.

Especially the sleeping.

The rest was needed, more than she knew. Another activity she eagerly sought? Taking a bath nearly every day. Soaking in the luxuriant bubbles soothed her frayed nerves and scrubbed off the lingering effects of living in squalor. Not only physically but in her mind. Chastity would never take tranquility for granted again.

During the week, she had hardly seen Ash except for two dinners with her and her family and another stroll along the street at dusk on one of the warmer evenings. He claimed he was very busy with various meetings and coming up with a plan to present to her regarding the future. Considering her confused and weary frame of mind, Chastity was glad to cede responsibility in this area, if only temporarily.

Regarding her brother and sister, there had been a further improvement in the look and actions of her siblings. The continued healthy eating and rest had put a rosy hue to their cheeks that Chastity had not seen in years.

Jon joined the dinner conversations more readily, and he did not glare at Ash with a churlish look any longer. Hannah acted more animated, and her enthusiasm for learning and reading made Chastity's heart ache with relief that life was heading on a more normal track.

How could she take them from this protective environment? Granted, they were here until Christmas, but what then? It was only a couple of weeks away.

What could she do? Be a paid companion? How?

Any potential employer would not accept her bringing her brother and sister. Do older ladies of the upper crust continue with paid companions any longer? It was undoubtedly a relic from another age, or so she assumed.

The only job she could think of paying enough to keep them within modest means? Employment at a fancy shop, like the ones on Bond Street. Could Ash arrange such a position?

Chasity heard a door slam. Ash was in his room. She tiptoed to the connecting door and laid her ear against it.

"You can come in, Chastity."

Her cheeks flushed hotly at being caught listening at his door. Turning the handle, she entered. "How did you know?"

"I saw your shadow under the door. Is there something you wish to discuss? I am joining my friends for dinner and cards later, but I have time for you."

Chastity sat in the chair by the fire. "We agreed that I would stay until Christmas. It's not far away. What then? I've been thinking."

Ash sat in the chair opposite. "Have you, indeed?"

She explained about the few positions she may be qualified for. At least ones that would allow her to keep her siblings with her.

"Is that your ambition to be a shopgirl in a fancy shop? And I am not looking down on it. If that is what you wish, it can be arranged."

"I don't know what I want, except for my brother, sister, and I to be comfortable and safe. Warm. We don't need much to live on."

"You can have that safe comfort—with me."

"There is something between us. I do not deny it. How could we make it work? A young woman from a dubious background, working in a shop, and a rich baron? It is not feasible."

"This isn't the Regency age, where everything is cloaked in manners and propriety. It will soon be eighteen ninety-eight. Society can still be harsh, but the impact has lessened and will continue to do so as we move into the new century. I don't give a hang what anyone thinks, at any rate."

Chastity heaved a sigh. "Not to be disrespectful, but you are in a position not to care what anyone thinks. I do not have that luxury. And while I appreciate everything you have done, we cannot stay here. Nor can we be seen in public with you again. It would excite comment, you know it. The carriage ride and dinner were not a good idea after all."

"So, we cannot build a relationship once you leave. What you are saying is that nothing can come from this mutual attraction. Do I have the right of it?"

"I-I-I suppose. I don't know. What do either of us know about relationships?"

Ash crossed his legs. "Beyond my parents' example? I can think of one that gave me a glimpse into what a relationship might entail."

"Please, tell me."

"At nineteen, I had a brief dalliance with the owner of a brothel. She schooled me on how to please a woman in bed. But before we entered such an intimate relationship, she made me take a vow. I would not share my knowledge unless it were with a woman of worth, a woman I cared for deeply. The thing is—I kept that vow. Most of my encounters with women were brief and—empty. Perhaps that's why I sought out sex in back alleys. To ensure it stayed devoid of emotion. It won't be like that between us. I know it. It hasn't been so far."

"I wish I had your confidence in the matter. Who was the owner of the brothel?"

Ash's look softened. "Her name was Christina. She was nineteen years older than me."

"My goodness. I thought you said you didn't have a mistress?" Chastity stated.

"I didn't. No money passed between us. It was more than a dalliance. It was an affair. The only one I ever had. Christina said, 'The sexual act is just that—an act. But when you share physical and intimate lovemaking with a person who has captured your heart, then anything is possible. The world is bright, your soul sings, loneliness slips away, for your heart is full. Even if it is of brief duration.'"

"That is quite the statement from a madam. You would think all romantic imaginings would have been driven from her years before," Chastity said, caught up in the story.

And how telling that he remembered what Christina had said, word for word.

"Yes, you would think that. Christina also said, 'Go and find the woman of your heart. You will know her. As soon as you lay eyes on her, you will know. Do not let her get away. Grasp life and love with both hands, Asher.' You know, Christina was right."

"How?" Chastity whispered.

"It's how I felt when I first laid eyes on you at the ball. I knew it," He laid his hand on his chest, above his heart. "Here. 'Don't let her get away,' but I did. You were gone, and I was miserable for a long time."

"Oh, Ash. Fate can be cruel, can't it?"

"Or not. It brought us back into each other's lives. It would be wrong not to explore what is between us. All I ask is that you not be so quick to dismiss it."

"You have a point. I will think about it some more, I promise. What happened with Christina?"

"When Christina told me of her romantic musings, I thought she spoke of a past love, but I realized she meant me. She was in love with me, and I had no earthly idea."

"Oh, no," Chastity gasped. "How tragic for her."

"Christina made the break claiming she had tired of me. Her rejection was not callous in nature but affectionate. After all, what would a woman of thirty-eight want with a young man of nineteen except a short-term affair? My younger self accepted her gentle rebuff with hardly a stutter of my heart."

Ash shook his head sadly. "By the time I stepped out into the hall to depart, I could have sworn I heard someone crying. It was Christina. How could I have been so callous and unfeeling? I had not meant to hurt her. I acted as a callow youth who had no clue of such deeper emotions. You see, the affair occurred not long after my mother died. I had already vowed not to allow emotion into my dealings with women. Even Christina gave me everything she had to offer, including her heart. And I presented nothing in return."

Chastity leaned forward and took Ash's hand. "I am certain that you didn't mean to hurt her. You were very young."

"I kept the vow all these years. It came to mean something to me. Christina deserved my promise and respect."

"You never saw her again?"

Ash rubbed the top of her hand with his thumb. "Some years later, I returned to the brothel to see how she faired, but they informed me she had sold the business a few months after she turned me out. They have no idea where she went or what became of her. I hope these last years have been kind to her."

"Grasp life and love with both hands. It is sound advice. It's also terrifying," Chastity murmured.

Ash sat forward, taking her other hand. "Here. We *can* grasp it with both hands. Like we are doing now. Together. We *can* have a future. Come to me when you believe it, too."

He kissed her hands, released them, then stood.

Chastity stood as well, though she grasped the arm of her chair as her legs were unsteady. Without replying, she returned to her room, gently closed the door, and leaned against it.

"Come to me when you believe it, too."

Oh, good heavens.

WARREN HAD RETURNED to Hertfordshire, and Brandon left the day before yesterday for Herne Bay. They were at their private club on Albany Street. Asher sat at the table with Gideon, Damon, Christian, and Merritt.

Christian had his talented cook, Mrs. Tallmadge, prepare a meal of roast chicken, baked salmon, and assorted side dishes. It had been delivered by coach by Christian's footmen.

"If you hold a dinner like this once a month, I would like to attend," Christian said as he twirled the stem of his wine glass. "But that is the extent of it."

"Yes, we understand, Christian. You are getting married. Bully for you," Damon said, with exasperation in his voice.

As usual, Christian ignored Damon's flippant remarks. "You all will attend our small wedding on Christmas day? I assure you it will be brief; there will be no sit-down meal. Merely a few Christmas treats like mince pies and mulled wine. It is what Eleanora wants."

"And what Eleanora wants—Eleanora gets," Damon replied.

Christian gave them a knowing smile. "Oh, indubitably."

"I would like to bring a guest if that is all right?" Asher said.

"Chastity Armitage?" Christian asked.

"Oh, God," Damon groaned, rolling his eyes.

"Who is Chastity Armitage?" Merritt asked.

"A young lady I once met at a ball. We have recently become reacquainted," Asher replied quickly.

He didn't want the rest of The Rakes to know about Chastity's story. He looked at Damon as if to say, 'keep your mouth shut.'

Damon merely snorted and took a drink of his whiskey.

"By all means, bring her along," Christian replied. "I would like to meet her, as would Althea and Eleanora."

"I will attend your wedding," Gideon pronounced. "I thank you in advance for keeping it small and brief. I loathe those tedious, long affairs with drawn-out wedding breakfasts and other dreary amusements."

Christian chuckled. "I am glad you approve."

"I've also been speaking to a few acquaintances concerning the dwindling membership of this circle," Gideon continued. "Damon has proposed changing the weekly meetings to monthly. I concur. When we convene in January, I will have four men with me. They are just sitting in, mind you. They will be prospects. One is Oliver Wollstonecraft, heir apparent to the Earl of Carnstone."

"He never contacted me about this," Asher murmured. He was slightly put out about it as he approached Oliver first.

"He had the sense that you were preoccupied," Gideon replied. "Miss Armitage, I presume?"

Asher didn't reply.

"Who else are you bringing, Watford?" Merritt asked.

"Troy Beckingham, Viscount Shinwell. He is the heir to the Earl of Darrington."

"Good Christ," Damon exclaimed.

"What? Someone you are intimately acquainted with?" Gideon questioned, giving Damon a sly but knowing grin.

"No comment. Move on. Who else?" Damon grunted.

"Gregory McFadden, owner of the Empire Business Group. He has his hand in newspapers, trains, and other concerns."

"Oh, wonderful. Another businessman," Damon groused.

"Yes, another businessman," Gideon snapped, showing a brief burst of emotion, which was unlike him. "Brandon recommended him; that's all I need to know. And the last one is Lord Romeo Linton, second son of the Duke of Coldbridge."

Merritt burst out laughing. "I say, who would name their son 'Romeo.' What lunacy."

"Don't tell Romeo that," Gideon replied. "The man is a talented boxer, built like a brick wall. You do not want to cross him. He goes by Rome. Any comment, Brookton? Perhaps you would prefer to handle recruitment."

"My mother is marrying Coldbridge," Christian said, chuckling. "A small world. I suppose that will make Coldbridge's two sons my stepbrothers."

The voices faded into the background as Asher realized he didn't give a hang about new members, marriages, or other points of contention.

All he wanted was to return home to Chastity.

Lord, he *was* in love.

Chapter 17

CHASTITY STOOD NEARBY, nervously watching as Doctor Corbett Buchanan examined Hannah. Ash had recommended the doctor. So far, he appeared competent enough. Doctor Buchanan worked with the police at the Bethnal Green Division.

Doctor Buchanan also had a small select group of patients. How interesting to find that he was Canadian. She had assumed he was from America, considering his lack of an English accent.

"Cough again, Hannah. That's it, thank you."

Doctor Buchanan was listening to Hannah's chest with a stethoscope. When finished, he motioned to the hallway, and Chastity followed him. When they were far enough away, he turned to face her.

"Do not despair. Hannah has nothing fatal. Put your mind at rest there."

Chastity shakily exhaled. "Oh, thank God."

"However, the long-term exposure to damp and cold conditions has affected her respiratory system. I detect a slight rattle. This means her bronchial tubes may have developed a permanent weakness. All that signifies is that she will be susceptible to lung infections. As long as she stays dry and warm and continues with a healthy diet, there is no reason she cannot live a long life."

Guilt speared Chastity.

Hannah had a damaged respiratory system because of her—and their hasty escape.

The doctor must have seen the anguish on her face, for he said, "It is not your fault. This is a common malaise, even among the upper echelons of society. London is a damp and chilly city. The fog exacerbates the condition."

"Would she be better off in the country?"

The doctor chuckled. "I believe we all would be better off, but time in the country may help in the short term; it is not a cure. The human body is an amazing machine. Damaged tissue can heal itself, given time and proper conditions. Already you said Hannah is not coughing as much?"

Chastity nodded.

"There you are. It is not serious; it is not life-threatening. Take comfort in that. Now, his lordship says I am also to examine you and your brother, Jon."

"Oh, yes, of course."

Thirty minutes later, the examinations were completed, with Doctor Buchanan giving Jon and Chastity a fair-to-improving bill of health.

The children returned to the schoolroom. Both were malnourished, though not horribly so, and a little underweight. Continued rest and healthy eating were recommended, including plenty of green vegetables, beef and fish, milk, eggs, and cheese.

Now sitting alone in her room, nursing a cup of tea, Chastity marveled that their conditions were not worse. Though they were bad enough.

If Doctor Buchanan had examined them when they first arrived at Ash's three weeks past, he would have reached a far different conclusion. As he said, the human body has an astonishing capacity to heal. Three weeks of healthy eating and rest had brought them to a "fair" overall diagnosis.

It proved that they could never find themselves in that position ever again. And speaking of situations, Chastity would have to find a secure and permanent one to ensure they stayed safe.

Images flickered through her mind of ghostly figures in a future time.

Chastity saw herself waiting in a room, reading. A few threads of gray were visible. Then Ash arrived, handsome as always. Even with the white at his temples and the wrinkles around his eyes and mouth.

He claimed he could only stay an hour as he must attend his son's eighteenth birthday party. In her daydream, Chastity had been his mistress for over twenty years. Still, he came to her. This would be her life, living for his brief stopovers.

Hannah and Jon had their own lives, but she would live only for Ash. When he left, she would weep. Bereft and alone, Chastity would reside on the peripheral edges of his life. A lamentable future—and not one she wanted.

Oh, good lord, what a dismal contemplation. What possessed her to imagine that dreary scenario? The future need not be so grim.

However, as a member of the peerage, Ash could never join her life to his since she'd been ruined beyond all expectations. Society would not tolerate such a match.

Or was he correct in stating that no one would care?

The only way she could share his life—according to society—would be as his mistress. And she couldn't and wouldn't do it.

Chastity should have never suggested it. It was not thought out and done in a state of desperation. But then, she never thought she would have feelings for the baron. Or ever dreamed she would fall in love with him.

Back to the hypothetical mistress scenario, not only would such an arrangement not be fair to her, but what about Ash's future wife?

And as far as Ash was concerned?

Chastity had the distinct impression that Ash would be faithful to his wife, regardless if it was a love match. So the mistress aspect was moot, thank goodness.

It was better that her heart was broken now than smashed to bits beyond repair over a lifetime. So, a tentative plan would be to depart right after Christmas and discover her own path for her and her siblings. If they had no future, it was imperative that she immediately shore up their plans.

Chastity vowed never to wait for any man. Nor would she live her life like a lonely character in a Dickens novel, with cobwebs and dust collecting about her person.

She had promised Ash she would think about there being something more between them. Chastity had thought of nothing else since they had the conversation. As difficult as it was to admit, she would have to explain to Ash that it was quite impossible; too many obstacles lay in their path.

Chastity could string Ash along, secure her family's future, and break all ties with him if she were devious.

Never. Ever.

Beaten down by life, Chastity couldn't bring herself to do such a horrendous thing.

But she would have to make him understand those obstacles.

Tonight.

ASHER STOPPED BY CLEVELAND Street as Althea stated she had further information regarding his case. Sitting in the study, he waited as patiently as he could for Christian and Eleanora's arrival.

"You don't mind that they are coming? They were part of the investigation," Althea asked.

"Do you mind having a duke trailing behind you and your sister and cousin, involving himself in your cases?" Asher replied, a smile on his face.

Althea laughed softly. "Christian is all in, in all ways. He and my sister are joined at the hip, and I have never seen them happier. I don't mind at all. He's quite good at investigating."

The couple strode into the room, and Althea was correct. They practically glowed with happiness. They sat close together on the sofa, causing Asher's smile to widen at the "joined at the hip" description. It certainly fits.

"Go ahead, Sister. It's your case." Eleanora said.

"Right. I met with Mr. Peebles, and we were able to locate the will together. I am sorry to say it was made *after* her marriage to Barrington. So, he is well aware of the contents. It was drawn up eleven months before her death. Mrs. Barrington must have known of her cancer diagnosis and wanted to see her children provided for."

Althea passed the single sheet of paper to Asher.

"There is also a guardianship agreement." Althea passed him another sheet of paper. "It is brief and to the point. The children are under his care until the age of twenty-one. The bond was waived as no money or property was left to the Armitage children."

Asher took that paper as well. He scanned the contents, and his heart sank. Straight to the point and brief indeed. The late Mrs. Barrington effectively signed her children over to Sir Nigel.

But then, what choice did she have? What choice did any woman have in such a circumstance?

"How disappointing," Eleanora said, frowning. "What did Mr. Peebles say about it?"

"Mr. Peebles has a suggestion, and I concur. He can draw up legal papers to have the younger Armitages' custody transferred to you," Althea stated.

Asher was shocked. "How? Why would any court allow a stranger to take custody of children from their stepfather? That's how a judge would see it. Again, we would have to reveal the repugnancy of Sir Nigel."

"Mr. Peebles stated that you could find a compassionate judge who would listen to your case privately and sign the papers then and there. I'm afraid Jon will have to tell this magistrate his story. Mr. Peebles has already reached out to one such empathetic justice," Althea said.

"But first, I need Barrington's signature before the court considers the legal transfer," Asher murmured.

"I'm afraid so," Althea replied. "I'm guessing Barrington won't sign, considering his loathsome nature."

"Then I will make certain he bloody well does sign it," Asher growled as fury burned within him. "Thank you, all of you. A brilliant job."

"What will you do, Asher?" Christian asked.

"See Mr. Peebles first to get those legal custody papers. Then, eventually, to Barrington. I won't mention it to Chastity and her siblings as yet. I don't want them to get their hopes up."

"Keep your temper, if you are able," Christian advised.

Not likely.

Not when he wanted nothing more than to pound the bastard into next week.

CHASTITY TOOK HER SUPPER in her room, waiting for Ash to return. He had been gone all day and even missed dinner. But around eight o'clock, she heard the door bang open and the heavy tread she had come to know as Ash's alone.

She knocked twice and, not waiting for a reply, entered his room, closing the door behind her.

There was no light in the room save the fire crackling in the hearth and a lone gas lamp on the sideboard. It reminded Chastity of the first night in his room, with only the moonlight filtering through the window.

Ash's bedroom possessed a definite masculine look with its large four-poster bed, walnut furniture, and dark wood panels on the wall. Earthy browns and tan colors accented the curtains, rugs, and upholstery. Elegant, tidy, and handsome, much like Ash himself.

All thoughts of conversation dissipated when he stood and faced her. Why was she here besides wishing to speak of the future? She set her doubts aside, at least for tonight. After what she'd been through the last three years, perhaps more than anything, she wanted to experience life and love, if only briefly.

Chastity cupped his cheek. "Let's not hold back, Ash. I want to feel. You make me—feel. Kiss me."

As she lowered her hand, Ash bracketed her face. His cognac-colored eyes glittered with a deep emotion that nearly seized her breath. Brushing his lips across hers with a feather-soft touch, he explored and nibbled her bottom lip, taking the kiss deeper by degrees. Chastity opened in an invitation, and he dove in, licking and tasting every inch of her mouth.

The kiss grew heated and urgent.

Ash slid his hands from her face to cup her behind, lifting and bringing her in against his erection. Through the layers of clothes, his heat and hardness were heady. Clasping his shoulders, she boldly tangled her tongue with his.

Moving away from her mouth, Ash laid hot kisses along to chin to her ear. "I could take you like this, standing upright if you wish. We don't even have to undress. I ache for you. I want to explore every part of you. Take my time and savor. What do you want, Chas? Tell me. I will do as you bid."

Against the wall reminded her too much of that horrid alley.

She closed her eyes and was transported back to the night she had surrendered her virtue for a bread crust.

That vile man.

She could not recall his face as she had kept her eyes closed tight, but she could smell him.

Urine and sweat had wafted off him and permeated her skin. She'd scrubbed herself raw for two days after, trying to remove his stink off her body. The man had roughly thrust into her. His rough and calloused hands had clasped her breasts; his foul breath had seared her cheeks and made her eyes water.

Chastity remembered the brief pain.

It had fueled the man's lust as he pounded and slammed her against the brick wall so hard it tore the back of her gown. Her customer had finished quickly, leaving her sticky, tossing coins at her feet as he stumbled drunkenly out of the alley.

"'ere's a couple o' extra for yer virgin cunny," he had called out.

Hannah had been horrified to discover various bruises when she helped scrub Chastity's back a few nights later. She had lied to her sister, stating she had slipped and fallen on the cobbles. It had taken her two months and another desperate need for money to have her venture back to the alley.

The second man was corpulent, his stomach all but suffocating his shaft. She slipped his pathetic appendage between her legs and moaned as if he had entered her. She'd seen other women in the alley do the same. He'd been so drunk he hadn't known the difference.

Oh, why did these terrible memories come back now? A sob escaped Chastity's trembling lips, her body going limp.

Ash stopped kissing her and stood back, his hands clutching her shoulders.

"What is it? Open your eyes, Chas."

Chapter 18

WHAT JUST HAPPENED?

Chastity had bloomed in his arms like the petals of an exotic flower, then, in increments, retreated. Chastity's eyes opened, and a lone tear trickled down her cheek. The misery on her face cut him to the bone.

"Shag Alley," she whispered miserably.

How could he be such an unfeeling sod? Of course, his vulgar pawing in this position would bring back her wretched recollections.

Asher lifted her into his arms and carried her to the bed. After he laid her on it, she turned on her side and curled into a ball. He lay beside her, gathered her close, and avoided pressing his shaft against her. Comforting her overrode his physical needs. Chastity did not sob hysterically but trembled nonetheless.

"You are safe here, my sweet. I vow it. I *am* sorry for suggesting sex against the wall. I wasn't thinking. Forgive me." He laid gentle kisses on her neck and cheek. "You are suffering from a past traumatic event. It still haunts you. Rest in my arms, and think of it no more."

Chastity sighed and snuggled closer. Asher had no idea of the time until the clock on the mantel struck nine. Close to an hour had passed. He had never held a woman like this. In a sheltering embrace for the sake of giving comfort.

Intimate warmth was a feeling new to Asher, and for the first time, he understood how two—a man and woman in love—became one. This revelation warmed him.

"I think I'm fine now, Ash," she murmured.

"I cannot begin to imagine what you have endured."

"I have had my fill of tragedy and heartache."

"I have no tragedy in my life except, as I mentioned, my parents dying far too soon. I was brought up in wealth and privilege; and, as you said before, denied nothing. Everything was handed to me because I was affluent and the son and heir of a well-respected baron. But I am not some brooding man without a heart or soul. I'm not tortured or damaged in any way." He paused. "But you are. Aren't you, Chastity?"

She nodded. "Yes, it appears I am. I did not know how much until you brought us here. On the streets, survival occupies your thoughts, your entire life. So much propriety falls to the wayside when you find you will do anything for a few coins. Since I've been here, it has given me time to reflect and remember. I want to forget." Chastity turned toward him, trailing her trembling fingers across his chest. "Make me forget, Ash. Make love to me."

"Are you certain? Perhaps it is too soon."

"I have never been certain about anything more in my life."

A giddy sort of bliss moved through him as he softly kissed her. She tasted of sweet regret and fiery passion. Asher moved lower, skimming his lips across her ample décolleté, pulling down the top of her gown to gain access to her breasts. Chastity surprised him by clasping a handful of the silk material and ripping it. With a husky sigh, he then deepened the kiss.

The moan that left his throat sounded as if it came from a wounded animal. He had secretly longed for a woman to be his equal in life, especially in the bedchamber. *My God, her passion matched his.*

He kissed her hard, then unfastened the first few hooks of her corset, pulling aside her chemise until her breasts were fully exposed.

Chastity gave a sensual, throaty laugh that hardened him further.

Asher lowered his head and suckled her breast, laving and licking until she writhed.

Chastity held his head in place, whispering hot demands in his ear.

He stood, tearing off his clothes and sending the garments careening about the room.

Waistcoat, shirt, trousers, smallclothes, shoes, and socks—gone instantly. If anything is ripped in the process, so be it. Naked and hard, Asher savored the beautiful vision laid out before him.

With one knee braced on the bed, he grasped the remains of her secondhand gown and ripped it to her ankles. She gasped and smiled as he tossed the ruined garment to the floor. His hands trembled as he separated the remaining hooks on her corset. All that remained were the gauzy chemise and her stockings.

With careful deliberation, he slowly rolled her stockings to her shapely ankles and then pulled them off, letting them flutter to the floor. The well-worn chemise came apart in his hands as she laughed. The joyous cadences of her amusement made his heart thump double-time.

She was so beautiful. Her skin seemed to shimmer in the firelight. Her gaze never wavered, nor did she hide the passion and sexual playfulness dancing in the depths of her beautiful eyes.

Asher would do as she asked and help her to forget.

Savor and love her as she deserves to be loved.

Cherish and protect her.

Asher took a few steps toward the sideboard and reached for the decanter of Madeira.

No time like the present to act out my fantasy.

He removed the stopper as he kneeled on the bed. With a teasing smile, he tipped the crystal decanter enough to allow a slow trickle of the Madeira to land on her chest.

Chastity squealed and jumped from the impact of the liquid. "Ash, the bedding!"

"I can afford to purchase new sheets. I want to lick every inch of your skin, drink, and delight in you."

Pouring a little more, he watched in fascination as the beverage ran rivulets over her beaded nipples and along her shapely torso.

Asher followed the sweet, sticky trail with his tongue, drinking and licking as he pursued the path to her midsection.

Chastity moaned and rolled her hips while spreading her legs further apart.

Asher curled his tongue and darted it into her navel, causing her to chuckle as he caught beads of wine in his mouth.

He tilted the decanter until another slow stream splashed on her stomach. More of the Madeira collected in her navel while the rest disappeared into her curls, wetting her.

Pouring some more, he leaned in, catching a few drops as they dripped over her thighs. He licked and sucked, drinking her essence, exploring every inch of her.

"Oh, Ash," Chastity groaned, her voice husky.

He bit down gently on her swollen nub and then flicked it with his tongue until she cried out with her release. Chastity's hips bucked on the bed; wine sloshed on the sheets. Her climax was the most beautiful thing he'd ever seen. Asher ached to be buried deep inside her.

Chastity gasped and then gave him a sensual look. "My lord, you are entirely wicked."

"I am that. You should know it."

He sat the near-empty decanter on the bed. The heady mixture of Chastity and the wine made his head swim; his blood thundered through his veins.

Asher wrapped his arms around her inner thighs and pulled her down closer until his face was buried in her feminine core. His tongue stroked her quivering nub over and over until another peak slammed her.

"And you learned all this from Christina?" she questioned as she curled beside him, trying to catch her breath.

"Yes. But know this. You *are* a woman of worth. Don't ever think differently. It is my fondest wish to be worthy of you." Asher pulled her closer.

Stroking his cheeks, she murmured his name affectionately. They lay in each other's arms for several minutes.

"I have another suggestion. Lay flat on top of me in the opposite direction. Slide down until your lips are inches from my cock."

"But then I will be above your face! No. It's too—"

"Wicked?"

"Intimate. Messy. And yes, wicked," Chastity replied somewhat primly.

"It's called *soixante-neuf,* oral sex in the sixty-nine position. Making love is intimate and messy but very gratifying."

"My, you did learn much from Christina."

"Yes. I am glad to be finally able to put this knowledge to good use. Do you trust me?"

She frowned as if weighing the question. "It appears my trust is important to you, as you have mentioned it more than once. It's hard for me to trust these past years. I do so *want* to trust you."

"Then, trust me."

A LEAP OF FAITH WOULD be required. Ash had been consistently honest and upfront with her from the moment they'd met, as far as she knew. What was wrong with giving each other mutual physical pleasure?

Nothing. Nothing at all.

She had come here to talk to him, but all thoughts of a drawn-out conversation had fled long ago.

She wanted to feel, to forget, so Chastity would do as he asked.

Ash spread his legs and bent them at the knee to give her greater access. Turning, she placed her knees on either side of his shoulders. What a strange position this was. He blew on her swollen folds, his warm breath causing her to shudder.

Fascinated, she trailed a finger around the many veins that encircled his shaft.

"Take me in your mouth," Ash murmured. "Suck and lick me. Make a feast of me, for I will be making a feast of you."

Ash buried his face between her legs, causing her back to arch. Chastity whimpered softly at the marvelous sensation.

Because of their height difference, she had to stretch to grasp his shaft. Placing it in her mouth, Chastity matched his rhythm. The air was filled with the sounds of their oral ministrations and passionate moans.

It took no time at all.

She came first with a blinding climax that nearly seized her breath. Dizzy from her release, she continued until, moments later, Ash groaned, shuddered, and called out her name.

Chastity turned about and curled up next to Ash again, laying her head on his shoulder.

They were covered in perspiration and breathing hard. Ash took her hand and laced his fingers through hers, placing them on his heart, which pounded hard and fast, matching her own heartbeat.

How greedy of her to want more. They hadn't even joined as yet tonight.

Ash kissed her forehead. "Rest. We have the rest of the night. I have so much more to savor. And so do you."

Chastity stifled a yawn as she was rather worn out. Ash reached for the sheet. The sweet smell of the Madeira surrounded them, the bedding decidedly damp from the wine and their sexual exertions.

Smiling and sated, she drifted toward slumber.

A stab of pain burrowed into her heart.

Ash would never be hers.

Only here, in bed. On this night.

Chastity wanted all of him: his body, regard, heart, and soul.

But I will never have it, will I?

Chastity exhaled sadly and then fell to sleep.

"Such a wonderful nap. I feel safe." Chastity ran her fingers through Ash's chest hair.

"No more worries tonight," he replied sleepily.

Chastity cupped his face. Ash's cheeks were flushed, his eyes sparkling and animated. The compassion and passion she read in his expression caught her breath.

All she had ever seen in a man's eyes was lust and a desire to control.

All she saw in Ash's hauntingly beautiful eyes was warm regard and affection.

Is it possible?

How deeply Chastity had slept while nestled in his embrace. To have that comfort always would be a blessing. A futile hope as this infatuation would not last, and she was not baroness material by any stretch of the imagination.

No choice but to savor these treasured moments.

"Stay," he rasped. "Sleep in my arms. All night."

How tempting.

"I better not. Hannah comes to my room in the mornings if I'm not there—"

He laughed. "Do you think the household is unaware of what we are doing? You, Chastity Armitage, are quite loud and expressive in your lovemaking."

"Me? You are even more so. Do you think we were heard? How undignified!"

Ash gave her a teasing wink. "Nothing undignified about finding pleasure with each other."

Chastity moved away, but Ash held her arms firm.

"Feel me. Feel how I respond to you. If I could, I would stay buried within you always. I sound mad."

No, she understood. But when a flame burns this intensely, it would flicker out sooner rather than later. She kept her observations to herself.

Enjoy. Savor. Make lasting memories.

It was all they could do.

That is why it remained imperative for her to focus on a method for her inevitable departure. She also must think of Jon and Hannah and their well-being.

"Not mad. Passionate. Love me one more time, Ash. Then I must take my leave."

After he rolled on a sheath, he laid her on her back, spread her wide, and thrust into her with a sure, slick glide. He growled and kissed her hard. And how she gave it back, each punishing thrust of his tongue, each exploration, and possession.

Chastity wrapped her arms and legs around his muscular body, raising her hips to meet him. As they climaxed together, a tear rolled down her cheek.

She was in love with Asher Colborne and would be until the day she died.

How could she stay?

But even more tragically, how could she leave?

Chapter 19

THE PAST TWENTY-FOUR hours could very well be the happiest of Asher's life. A warm glow still covered him from last night's passionate encounter.

But today was a new day, and he had much to accomplish.

The new wardrobes had arrived a short while ago, and Asher smiled at Hannah's delighted cries at the sight of her new dresses. Jon had already thanked him for his new wardrobe as well. As a young man of fourteen, soon to be fifteen, it was time Jon owned proper trousers, waistcoats, and jackets.

Chastity pulled Asher to the corner of the room. "Thank you for all of this, for Hannah and Jon. And especially for me. My gowns are beautiful. And so many fancy undergarments?"

"You will model each one for me. Privately."

Chastity blushed prettily. How tempting to ask her to model the garments at this very moment.

However, other items on his agenda needed to be addressed. Asher squeezed her hand affectionately, then turned and left the sisters to enjoy their new wardrobes.

How satisfied he felt at giving them something as essential as clothing. At times it was easy to forget that many went without.

One of the first things he did this morning? He sent a note to Christian, asking if he could be included in any plan to craft future legislation regarding the rights of women, children, and the poor.

Christian had immediately replied that he welcomed his assistance and would send word when he was ready to meet with like-minded peers like Carnstone and Gransford.

After taking his leave from Chastity and her sister, he instructed the carriage driver to head to Mr. Peebles's office. Yesterday, after his meeting with The Galway Agency, Asher had sent word to Mr. Peebles to have the custody papers ready.

He strode into the office and was escorted to Mr. Peebles immediately.

"Ah, my lord. Do take a seat. I have news. Magistrate William Bellows has agreed to hear your case in his private chambers Tuesday next, at three in the afternoon. Jon Armitage and the eldest sister will be required to testify. He is sympathetic to our cause as I explained certain generalities of the situation."

Asher hadn't counted on Chastity having to give testimony, but logically, it made sense.

"I'll ensure that they are in attendance. What about Barrington's signature? Is it needed?"

Mr. Pebbles pushed his spectacles against the bridge of his nose. "It would no doubt make the case stronger."

"Won't Magistrate Bellows need to hear Barrington's side of it?"

"Not if you have the signature, my lord. I informed the judge that the children were traumatized and must not be in Sir Nigel's presence. Bellows cannot abide children being mistreated in any way. As I said, he is sympathetic."

Asher took the papers and flipped through them. "Good God, what a bunch of legal jargon."

"But much needed. If you look at that paragraph there, my lord," Mr. Peebles leaned forward and pointed. "I stated that Mrs. Barrington was unwell and under duress when the will was drawn up, that she had no other recourse but to choose her husband as guardian. I also stated that she was unaware of her husband's predatory interest in the children."

"Well done, Mr. Pebbles. Comprehensive, as usual." Asher folded the papers and tucked them inside his coat. "I am heading to Barrington's now. The sooner we obtain the signature, the better."

"And if he won't sign?"

"Oh, he will," Asher said, his voice determined.

Peebles stood and held out his hand. "Then I will meet you Tuesday next at the magistrate's office, my lord. I will send a message soon with the address."

Once out in his carriage, he blew out an exasperated breath. Asher would have to keep his temper under a tight rein and not give too much away initially. An experienced gamester revealed his hand when he was assured of winning.

CHASTITY LEFT HANNAH in her room, surrounded by new clothes and books. She had never seen her sister so happy. It gave her such a warm feeling to know her siblings were thriving. What a difference from a month ago.

As she headed toward the small library next to the study, she met Grimes in the hallway.

"Have you seen the baron?" she asked.

"I believe his lordship stated he had several appointments with his solicitor and one with a Sir Nigel Barrington, Miss Armitage."

Chastity's blood froze in her veins.

He wouldn't.

Barrington? To what purpose? After everything that she'd confessed, Ash would meet with that deviant.

Panic clutched her insides as a knot formed in her stomach. And why did the butler tell her of Ash's exact schedule? Chastity glanced at

Grimes. The man gave her a polite smile. He treated her as if she were the lady of the house, which was an absurd conclusion.

"Thank you, Grimes," she managed to croak.

The butler gave a slight bow and continued along the hallway.

Her emotions ran amuck, completely untethered. The proof lay in the fact that her heart pounded fiercely in her chest, her breathing became ragged, and her inner thoughts sounded irrational to her own ears. Dizziness overcame her, so Chastity halted and leaned against the wall until it passed.

But it didn't matter if her thoughts were illogical. Pure fright urged her onward.

Chastity turned and ran for the stairs. Once in the upper hall, she threw open the door to Jon's room. He lay on his bed reading a book. Quietly, she closed the door and leaned against it.

"We have to leave," she whispered harshly.

Jon sat bolt upright. "What? Why? What has happened?"

"Baron Wenlock has gone to Sir Nigel this very afternoon. He will be handing you and Hannah back into his custody."

Jon stood, the book dropping to the floor. "The baron said that? I can't believe it."

Chastity's mouth dropped open in shock. "Since when are you a champion for Wenlock?"

Jon frowned. "Since when are you not?"

"We must flee. I will not have you and Hannah returned to Barrington," she cried in a hoarse whisper. "I will not have us separated after everything we've been through!"

"W-w-we can't leave! You said we would be here until after Christmas—" Jon sputtered.

"Hang it all! Let me think. I have nine pounds from that first night. The baron gave me ten pounds of pin money last week. We can take these new clothes and sell them—"

Jon grabbed her arms and shook her. "Sister, you are not making any sense! I just spoke to the baron a few days ago. He promised to look after us and see that I am educated at good schools so I can join the law. Are you telling me that he lied? About all of it?"

Chastity rubbed her forehead as a dull ache pounded behind her eyes. She could not think straight or catch her breath.

Why would he tell Jon such a fabrication? Or was it a fabrication?

Her mind swirled in confusion. The room began to spin again as her fright instinct notched up another level.

"The baron made me promise to look after you and Hannah, and I gave him my word," Jon continued when she didn't reply. "How can I do that if we leave? How can I acquire a good education and occupation if we take to the streets again?" Her brother gave her another shake. "Look at me!"

"You never told me of this conversation," Chastity whispered.

And neither had the baron.

"Well, I'm telling you now."

Taking a deep breath and exhaling, she cupped Jon's cheeks. "How can we trust anyone? Think of what Sir Nigel put us through. The law is on *his* side; the baron told me as much! Our stepfather has a legal claim and can take you and Hannah back without a by-your-leave. Wenlock is probably making arrangements to hand us over as we speak."

Since when had she ever referred to Ash as Wenlock or the baron? It was as if he had become a stranger to her. How disturbing. Chastity shook away the observation.

All that mattered was getting her siblings to safety.

"So, you don't actually *know* why his lordship went there? Shouldn't we wait and hear his side?" Jon questioned. "You're not thinking rationally."

Chastity trembled in fear. How dare Jon gainsay her? Her brother made sense for a brief second, but then her fear took possession of her, fueling her flight sense. Yes, they must flee immediately.

"No. I will *not* wait. I should have never revealed as much as I did to the baron. Gather some clothes and be quiet about it, or the governess and other servants will hear us. We have to sneak out somehow. Do it, Jon!" She broke from his grip. "I'll return shortly, be ready to depart. I have to pack for Hannah, and don't you dare tell her what is going on."

Chastity left the room and ran to hers, closing the door. Her hands trembled so much that Chastity could barely grasp the door handle. Her heart was beating far too fast.

This time, she would not depart without a few trinkets to barter. Chastity tiptoed into Ash's room, found a carpetbag, then began to fill it with anything of value she could lay her hands on.

Chapter 20

ASHER PATTED HIS SIDE pocket where the document lay. Deciding against a drink—though he could use one—his carriage delivered him to the modest residence of Sir Nigel Barrington.

It would be prudent to stay on his guard and bank his temper. Once shown into the man's study, Asher gazed out the window, waiting for his arrival.

Jon's stark admission still haunted him. No wonder they had all fled.

Wearing a respectable black wool suit, Sir Nigel strode into the room with an arrogance that annoyed Asher immediately. He was trim, healthy, and comfortable in his own skin. The gray at his temples and the few wrinkles around his eyes showed the man could be in his mid-forties or older.

"Have we met, my lord?" Sir Nigel asked with detached politeness. Barrington offered a limp and clammy handshake. Asher fought to keep the distaste from his face.

"We have. It must be close to three years past. I came to inquire after Miss Chastity Armitage. I am to understand that you are her guardian. Or was, I assume, that she is past the age of majority by now."

The man did not even bat an eyelash. Asher watched as recognition dawned on the emotionless face.

What disturbed Asher was Barrington's eyes. They were lifeless, devoid of warmth, and black as midnight. Very eerie, indeed. As if evil is lurking below the surface.

"Would you care for a drink, my lord?" Barrington offered, not bothering to acknowledge Asher's statement.

"No."

Hang politeness and parlor manners.

Barrington motioned to a nearby seat, then sat across from him. "The chit caught your eye at a ball if I recall."

"You possess a sharp memory, Sir Nigel. I am afraid every young lady I have encountered since then pales in comparison. I wondered if you would be so kind as to furnish me with her address in Scotland. I plan a trip north soon and thought I would call upon her. Perhaps she will consent to me courting her."

Asher threw in a brief but fake-polite smile, but it was damned hard to hold his tongue—and his ire.

Barrington crossed his arms. "Made that much of an impression, did she?"

"Quite. I thought it prudent to seek you out to make my request. Therefore, why I am here to ask permission. You are Miss Chastity's stepfather, after all."

Asher gave him another brief smile, but this one held no faux warmth or warmth of any kind.

"Well, my lord, I cannot, in good faith, hand out an address to just anyone, baron or no. I have an alternate proposal. I will write the dear girl and ask if she would be receptive to an introduction."

Smooth and sly response, dripping with disdain.

Asher knew what would transpire next. Barrington would allow a few months to pass and then regret to inform him that Chastity Armitage did not want to meet him.

So sorry, old chap.

Miserable bastard.

"That is not an answer I will accept," Asher replied in a deadly tone.

Barrington shrugged. "The Armitage children are under my care as per the wishes of my dear late wife. It would be a decided insult to her precious memory to cavalierly toss her oldest daughter to a baron for his amusement. Find another pretty chit to fuck. My lord."

The "my lord" was said with a sneer.

Precious memory, my arse.

Asher's parents had brought him up to be a gentleman. But it was becoming impossible to keep that gentlemanly veneer in place. Asher clenched his fists, aching to leap from his chair and pound that smug face into a pulpy mess.

Barrington purposely provoked him. Why? A test of some sort? Or perhaps Barrington was so arrogant that he had no idea of the danger he was in.

"How long is the term of your guardianship? What stipulations were placed? You seemed to have neglected your duty by fostering them off on distant relatives in the wilds of Scotland," Asher said, struggling to hide his growing fury.

"What matter is that to me? They are not my blood. Leave your address, and I will write the girl. I can do no more than that," Barrington sniffed haughtily.

Asher pulled the document from his pocket and held it between his fingers.

"Sign custody over to me of the Armitage children, and I promise that I will not report to Scotland Yard how you abused Jon with your unwanted, amoral advances and threats toward the girls."

Sir Nigel's eyes narrowed, but he did not respond.

Asher gave Barrington a deadly look. "I am a peer of the realm. I can request and receive an audience with the queen. My family is well known to the royal family and especially Her Majesty. The audience would be granted promptly because of more than three hundred years of faithful service by the Colborne family."

"So? What do I care?" Sir Nigel snapped.

"You must be aware of how Queen Victoria feels about sexually deviant behavior. You will have your knighthood stripped and be tossed into Newgate Prison for the rest of your life."

Barrington's onyx eyes shone with malice. "Clever. You knew all along they were not in Scotland. Where ever did you find them? It must be a juicy tale. I do not need to sign the document. Marry the obstinate bitch, and custody will revert to you as her husband. It's in the blasted will. If you want the Armitage brats, you have your answer." Sir Nigel gave him a self-righteous look.

Asher had seen the will and studied it. Nowhere did it mention that custody reverts to Chastity. Another lie. He remained silent, but inside; Asher seethed with a rage that bordered on murderous.

"But who needs marriage; make her your mistress," Sir Nigel continued. "I'll bet her juicy cunny is quite glorious. I'll bet you've been between her thighs already. That good, was she? She never was to my taste. I like mine younger and prettier. Jon is a pretty lad. Have you had him, too?" Sir Nigel sneered leeringly. "And I imagine Hannah is coming along nicely."

Asher's livid gaze locked with Barrington's. The man wore a lascivious grin on his face. Mentioning the word mistress concerning Chastity was terrible enough. But to mention Jon in such a way? And Hannah?

To hell with it. I'll beat him to a bloody pulp.

There was no containing his rage; it spilled over, smothering all restraint. Damn the man's eyes for the insult to Chastity and his leering comment about Jon. All his gentlemanly upbringing had fallen to the wayside.

Asher shot out of his chair and grabbed Sir Nigel by the cravat, slamming him to the floor. A decided crack could be heard as his fist slammed into Sir Nigel's nose. Blood sprayed onto Barrington's waistcoat and dribbled down the man's chin. Sir Nigel whimpered as Asher continued to batter his face.

The butler opened the door and gasped in shock. He must have heard the whimpers turn into screams.

Asher stood, looking down at the pathetic beast writhing and crying on the floor.

Asher glanced at his hands; they were bloody. A tooth was embedded in one of his knuckles.

"Fetch Sir Nigel a physician. He's had an accident."

When the butler quietly closed the door, Asher continued his assault without a flicker of guilt.

Chapter 21

CHASTITY SLIPPED ON her wool cloak and then grasped the overloaded carpetbag. Besides the trinkets, she stuffed some gowns and dresses into a sack to sell later.

The bits she had collected were light enough to carry and would fetch needed coins. Inside the bag were three china figurines, two silver dishes, a mother-of-pearl hand mirror, fancy linens, and towels.

Also in the sack was twenty-one pounds, which would be more than enough to get them far away from London. They could find employment on a farm, doing what she had no idea about, but departing the city must be their first priority.

On her bed lay a green evening gown. Sighing, she trailed her fingers across the garment, reveling in the sensual feel of the silk. She would never own anything as beautiful again. Glancing at the other pieces of clothing on the bed, she choked back a sob. Ash must have spent a fortune. The extravagance!

Her rational mind said: *Why would the man spend such vast amounts of money if he was planning to return you all to Sir Nigel?*

But coherent and sensible thoughts were not ruling her now; she ran on pure, unadulterated fright.

Chastity touched the gold corset. Last night had been incredible; the gentle and tender way Ash comforted and loved her would stay with her for the rest of her days.

Again, she ignored her rational mind: *Why would he treat you lovingly if he planned to betray you?*

Nothing mattered, not common sense, rational thought, or her love for Ash.

All she could focus on, all she could think of? —to escape.

To protect her siblings.

Chastity wiped a wayward tear from her cheek as she sprinted toward the door. But she stopped in her tracks.

Wait. What in the world was Chastity doing?

Thieving? Running?

How could she subject Jon and Hannah to life on the streets again, moving to ramshackle rooms and trying to find employment? It was no kind of life; she knew that. But neither was handing her siblings over to Barrington.

She rubbed her forehead, confused, scared, and feeling more than a little foolish. Jon must think she had lost her mind.

Perhaps she had.

There had to be a logical explanation for all this. Ash mentioned last night that she suffered from a traumatic event. It obviously had affected her far worse than she believed. This reaction was definitive proof. At least some common sense finally broke through the cracks.

Chastity could hide the bags, wait for Ash's side of the story, and if they still had to depart, she would be packed and ready to leave at a moment's notice.

This plan made much more sense than fleeing outright, at least in this circumstance.

Chastity rubbed her eyes, then looked up. Ash stood in the doorway. He was pale, his eyes a little wild. Blood dripped from his handkerchief-wrapped hand, and crimson spatters dotted his waistcoat.

Chastity cried out, dropped the carpetbag and sack, and ran to his side. Carefully, Chastity lifted his swollen and bloody hand. One knuckle was split and bleeding profusely. Bruises already rose to the surface of the skin.

"Ash, what happened?"

He seemed to be in a daze.

"Are you going somewhere?" His gaze slid to the bags. "You are leaving me?" Ash stumbled.

Sliding her arm about his waist, she led him to the nearby chair. Worriedly, she ran to the basin and poured fresh water into it. Chastity placed it on the table next to the chair, then knelt at his side.

Ash remained stock-still and eerily silent.

How interesting that as soon as she saw Ash in disarray, in torment, she ran to his side and offered her assistance. The remainder of her thoughts of escape had fled. However, she had decided to wait just before Ash appeared.

"Oh, Ash. Please tell me what occurred!" She dipped the cloth in the water and dabbed at the blood.

"I paid Sir Nigel a visit. We had a slight disagreement," he replied hoarsely.

Slight?

Sir Nigel must not have landed any punches, as Ash's face remained free from any sign of a struggle. Ash reached into his side pocket with his free hand, wincing at the pain. He held folded papers out to her.

"I made certain that Barrington could grip a pen, though barely. He signed over custody of your brother and sister to my keeping. Your family is free from Sir Nigel. On Tuesday next, we need to meet privately with Magistrate Bellows, and the agreement will be notarized and legal. Mr. Peebles, my solicitor, arranged it."

The shock caused her to drop the cloth and reach for the parchments with both hands. They trembled as she unfolded it and read through the paragraphs.

There was a lot of legalese she had no clue about, but sure enough, at the bottom of the page, the shaky signature of Sir Nigel Barrington stood out.

The two drops of blood near the name were particularly chilling.

But Chastity felt no remorse.

Barrington deserved the beating. More even, in her mind.

"I tried to keep my temper, but it was a miserable failure. I beat the man quite bloody. I had not lost control like that before, and while the prospect disturbed, it was also damned satisfying," Ash rasped.

"You did this for me—for all of us?" she whispered. "What does it mean?"

"The children are under my care until they reach the age of majority. It is legal. My solicitor ensured it would stand up to official scrutiny after the judge signs off on it."

Ash shifted in his seat and groaned in pain. Chastity laid the papers on the table, then continued to blot away the blood on his hand.

"I had Barrington investigated and the will and testament located. Did you know what your mother died of?" Ash asked.

"No. Everything happened within such a short period. I know Mother hadn't been well for months. I assumed it was melancholy. My mother died one day after I attended the ball. The following three weeks after her death until we escaped are a blur to me."

"The investigative agency discovered her medical records. Your mother had cancer of the stomach and had known about it for some time."

Chastity felt her insides knot as tears formed. "I had no idea. She suffered silently; I believe Barrington had no idea either. Unless he didn't care, which is possible. Oh, my poor mother. We never had a chance to mourn her properly. I resented her for marrying Barrington." She swiped away a tear. "I soon learned what sacrifice meant and what my mother endured to keep us safe. What was in the will?"

"Knowing she was fatally ill, your mother made Sir Nigel guardian."

"I wish she had told me," Chastity said softly. "But what choice did she have?" Everything fell into place. How was her mother to know Barrington would immediately prey on her children?

Oh, Mother, forgive me for thinking ill of you.

"Speaking of choices, why were you leaving? Tell me, Chastity."

"I-I-I asked Grimes where you had gone, and when he mentioned Sir Nigel's name, I'm afraid I reacted rather desperately. Oh, Ash, I thought you arranged to hand us back to that vile man, or at least Jon and Hannah."

The hurt expression on his face caused a few tears of regret to bead on her eyelashes.

"I should have told Grimes not to repeat it." Ash frowned. "After everything you have told me, after all that we have shared, you truly believed that I would be callous enough to do such a horrid thing? Did you not tell me that you trusted me with your very life and with the lives of Jon and Hannah? And this is how you react?"

Chastity could hear the incredulous agony in his voice, and she rested her head on his lap.

"Please, forgive me, Ash. I can't explain why I reacted so. Deep down, I do trust you. Yet, cold fear gripped me and would not let go; it pushed out any rational thought. I am sorry. I can only suggest that it's living on the street and always seeing danger at every turn. My flight predisposition took over."

He said nothing at first, then soothingly touched her hair.

"I believe I can understand. You told me it was hard to trust, and I cannot blame you after what you have been through. I should have informed you of my plans, but I wanted to be certain of the details first. But you should have given me the benefit of the doubt."

Chastity nodded, sniffling. "I know. Jon told me such in no uncertain terms. I have been more deeply affected by the past few years than I originally thought. I acted illogically. Forgive me?"

"Yes. Of course," Ash said softly.

A knock sounded at the door. The door opened, and Jon and Hannah peeked around the edge.

"May we come in?" Jon asked tentatively.

"Yes," Chastity replied.

"Oh," Hannah gasped. "Are you all right, my lord?"

"Yes. Come here, children." They came to stand before Ash. "I visited Sir Nigel. We had words, and I beat him rather badly."

"Good," Jon growled. "I'm glad of it."

"Well, I am not glad that I lost all control. And violence is not something I condone. It is not like me at all. But in this case, the end justifies the means."

Ash reached for the papers. "I forced Sir Nigel to sign this. It reverts custody of you both—to me. But there is one final legal step to make it permanent. Jon, you and Chastity must attend a private meeting with Magistrate Bellows next Tuesday. My solicitor will also be there, as will I. You will have to tell him exactly what you told me. Can you do that?"

Jon looked at Chastity. "I didn't want you to know. I didn't want to worry you." Jon then turned to face Ash. "I will tell the judge. If it means we never see our stepfather again, I will tell him everything."

"Good man. I've been thinking. I cannot keep you all hidden away in this house for eternity. We should see to your re-entry into society, come up with an explanation for your absence, and a solid, rational reason you are all with me."

"Thank you, my lord," Jon smiled.

"Yes. Very well. Take your sister to the parlor. We will be there directly," Ash replied wearily.

Hannah ran and kissed Ash on the cheek, then Jon took her hand, and they left the room.

Chastity sat back and looked up at Ash. "I was hardly 'out' in society—a few weeks at best. Besides, you have done so much already. How we can repay you, I do not know."

"I did not do this for payment or praise," Ash replied quietly.

"I know. I do not wish to be seen as an object of pity. Or as a victim. I am not a weak woman, yet I cried and trembled in your arms last night. Look how I reacted this afternoon. Perhaps I'm not as strong as I believe."

"May I think of you with admiration for your bravery? For having the intestinal fortitude to do what had to be done to keep you all safe and alive?" Ash caressed her cheek briefly with the tips of his fingers.

"There is no place I would rather be than here—with you," Chastity spoke the truth. "For however long that is. Until Christmas or whenever you say."

"With custody of Jon and Hannah, there is no need for any of you to go anywhere."

"At some point, you will marry. You will not want us underfoot. I understand that."

She might comprehend it, but it tore her in two to think of him with another woman. But until then, Chastity would love him with everything she had.

"Reach in my coat pocket."

Chastity set aside the cloth, tunneled her hand in his right pocket, and pulled out a small blue velvet box. Inside was a gold cross with a small diamond, like the one her parents had given her long ago. Opening it, she gasped.

"I am not certain if it is similar to the one you had to sell, but I wanted you to have a suitable replacement," he murmured.

"Oh. It's beautiful. Thank you," Chastity whispered, a lump of emotion lodging in her throat.

"There is something else I want. More than I want to take my next breath. Would you consent to be my wife?"

ASHER WAITED FOR HER answer. He shocked her. Asher wanted her with him always, at his side and in his bed.

He loved her.

Completely and without prejudice.

Chastity was the very air he breathed.

Before meeting with Mr. Pebbles and going to Barrington's, he had slipped into the nearby jewelers on a whim, hoping to find a necklace like the one she'd described. While there, he had also looked at wedding rings.

Asher couldn't wait to bring her back to the shop so they could pick out their wedding rings.

That is if she agreed.

After she'd left him at two in the morning, he'd lain awake the rest of the night and had formulated his plans. Their sweet and heated lovemaking finally brought his emotions into clear lucidity.

Since he reached the age of majority, he had behaved like other young men in his sphere.

His father had never admonished him for his wicked ways. Asher wished now he had. There was much to make up for.

This lovely, courageous woman, whom he loved fiercely with all his heart, deserved his respect.

Chastity remained silent, still staring at the necklace, so he forged ahead.

"I will take you all to Wenlock Manor and out of the temporary scrutiny of society. The children can continue their lessons, and I will tell all and sundry that I met you at the ball three years ago and could not get you out of my mind. I've already told my friends that fact. It is not a lie. You have haunted my thoughts many a night since I first laid eyes on you."

Asher gave her a warm smile. "We began a correspondence, and now I have brought you here from Scotland to be my wife. I will hire a chaperone immediately. In society's eyes, your reputation will be unstained. Sir Nigel will not say a word except to back up my story. He knows what will happen if he does not."

Chastity said nothing, just continued to stare at the jeweler's box in her hand.

"My love, have I shocked you into stupefaction?" Asher asked, his voice soothing.

"You cannot marry me. I am not suitable. I sold myself—"

Asher clasped her arms and lifted her into his lap. He gently stroked her cheek with the back of his fingers.

"No one outside your family is aware of that fact, and no one will *ever* find out. Not even Barrington knows."

Chastity gazed up into his eyes. "But *you* know."

"And you think that will be a barrier between us? Never. My brave lady, I love you. Absolutely worship you. I think I have from the moment I saw you at the ball. I did not know how much until I brought you here. I want you to be my wife, lover, and dearest friend."

He kissed her pale cheek. "Hannah and Jon will want for nothing. In fact, I've already spoken to Jon about going away to school shortly. He is quite keen. Why not attend Oxford University when the time comes if he does well?"

Asher gave her a reassuring smile. "Jon will be fine, Chastity. Put any worries from your mind. Your worst fears did not come to pass. He confided the particulars to me. He's a valiant lad and ready to move forward with his life. Are you ready to move forward with yours? Can you trust me?"

She did not answer, but he could see tears gathering on her golden lashes again.

He continued, "Hannah will have a proper coming out. If she grows as beautiful as you, she will have a line of suitable beaus queuing up to court her. I will see to it she has a generous dowry—"

Chastity laid a finger against his lips to silence him. "You love me?"

"With all my heart and soul. With every fiber of my being. To the very marrow—"

Chastity kissed him with an aching passion that vibrated through him and joined his own. The kisses grew frantic until, at last, Chastity pulled away, laid the jeweler's box in her lap, then cupped his cheeks with her trembling hands.

"I love you too, Ash. Quite desperately. And I promise to trust you in all things. I will marry you, do whatever, or say whatever it takes. Last night I had vowed to myself that I would leave after Christmas. I did not want to be hurt because I had fallen deeply in love with you. Will this work?"

"My sweet, yes. We are perfect for each other. You are the woman of worth I have been waiting for."

She embraced him tight. "Thank you for Jon and Hannah. They are fond of you already. How could they not? Jon spoke quite vehemently in your defense. I suppose we should pack for Wenlock Manor."

"Before we leave at the end of the month, I wish to attend a small wedding for my friends, Christian and Eleanora. You will like them. I've already asked if you can attend, and they wholeheartedly agreed. It is on Christmas Day, a few hours at most."

"Oh, a wedding. I would love to come with you and meet your friends."

Asher laughed and nuzzled her neck, whispering words of love in her ear.

He absolutely adored her.

His love—his life—forever.

CHRISTMAS DAY 1897

AS CHRISTIAN STATED, the wedding was a small affair in the parlor of Christian's town house. In attendance were The Rakes of St. Regent's Park, Christian's mother, the Duchess of Allenby, her intended, The Duke of Coldbridge, Althea Galway, and her cousin, Sybil Norton. Also, there was Doctor Buchanan, Archie Fitzgerald, and Mrs. Bartle, the Galway's housekeeper. Reece Galway, uncle, and police sergeant walked Eleanora down the aisle.

On a side table, many food items were laid out. Mince pies, apple tarts, gingerbread, small sandwiches, rum punch, mulled wine, coffee, tea, and decanters of spirits. Next to the table, an elaborately decorated Christmas tree with lit candles gave the room a festive and romantic look. Eleanora wore a red velvet gown with a matching fur-lined cape. She had pieces of holly in her bouquet of white roses and her fashionable upswept hair. Christian wore a black suit with a holly corsage.

As Christian and Eleanora exchanged vows before Reverend Farrell, Asher took Chastity's gloved hand and slipped it into his. She looked up at him and smiled.

"This spring," he whispered in her ear so no one else could hear, "That will be us. Early spring, I hope."

Chastity squeezed his hand. "Very early spring."

Asher glanced about the room. Gideon looked somewhat bored, but standing next to him? Damon did not. Damon kept his gaze firm on Althea, only looking away when she glanced his way. Something was brewing there, it may percolate for a time, but Asher did not doubt that it would bubble over at some point.

His friends deserved contentment—the true rakes among them most of all. None of them were getting any younger. Gideon would be 40 years old next month. Christian found his love, and Asher had found his. Here's hoping the rest found happiness in a timely manner.

Chastity came back into his life through a twist of fate, providence, or whatever else to call it. He would make it his life's work to see all the Armitages were safe, happy, and well-loved. Especially Chastity.

Happy endings existed, after all.

Epilogue

WENLOCK MANOR
   Summer 1908
   In the decade since they married, Asher and Chastity had spent most of that time at Wenlock Manor, only going to London a few months at a time when Parliament sat.
   Asher had been given custody of Jon and Hannah, and Asher and Chastity were married in London in the early spring of 1898.
   Chastity and her brother and sister had thrived in the past years.
   Jon Armitage, now twenty-four, was a successful barrister living and working in London's west end. Jon was a young partner in a prestigious firm and opened a small law clinic in the East End, offering free legal advice to those who could not afford it.
   Hannah, twenty-one, had grown into a beauty just as Asher had predicted. She had several young men interested, but she favored Oliver Wollstonecraft's younger brother, Bryan. Although, Asher had noticed sparks flying between Hannah and Archie Fitzgerald, the former ward of his friend, Christian. Archie was the manager and head investigator of The Galway Investigative Agency.
   Hannah had recently sold a column to a lady's magazine, and there was a good chance it would become a monthly feature.
   As for Asher, he had never been happier.
   He was still a member of The Rakes of St. Regent's Park, as the club of men had turned their objectives to a more worthy pursuit. When in

London, he met with his friends, former rakes all, but life at Wenlock Manor is when he felt truly content.

Especially his life with Chastity.

They had two children, a girl, Celina, aged eight, and a boy, Newton, aged five. They were the joy of Asher's life.

Chastity rushed into his study. "Ash, I am not sure we will be ready to leave on time. Newton is complaining of a toothache."

Asher smiled. "I can send word to Christian and Eleanora; they won't mind if we are a couple of days late."

For the past several years, Christian Bamford, The Duke of Allenby, and his wife, Eleanora, invited family and friends to Bamford Park for two weeks of sun, picnics, and other entertainment.

The large estate was packed to the rafters but also filled with joy. He was looking forward to seeing all the rakes, especially Brandon Knight. The two men had become good friends through the years, seeing that their paths to true love had similar obstacles.

Asher pulled Chastity close. She had only grown more beautiful if that were possible. He trailed the tip of his finger across her cheek. All vestiges of her wretched past had disappeared.

The weary, haunted look and, more importantly, the anxiety had dissipated. It had taken a while for all the Armitages, but they had moved on.

As for Sir Nigel Barrington, Asher let it be known to Queen Victoria what Sir Nigel had put his stepchildren through. She immediately stripped him of his honorific.

When the queen died in 1901, Barrington appealed to King Edward, Victoria's son, to have the knighthood restored. He was categorically refused.

It was decided that bringing criminal charges would be fruitless and more damaging to the children. Asher did pursue it quietly, for why should such a man be allowed to walk free? But more than one barrister said the publicity would be vicious.

Sadly, the conviction rate was low, and the child victims were often seen as fallen, morally corrupt, and a threat to society. It made Asher's blood boil. Besides, Jon had asked him not to go any further with it.

The last Asher heard of Barrington?

The miserable bastard had sold his small town house and left for America. Good riddance.

Chastity snuggled close to him. "Jon has sent word he will be joining us on our holiday to Bamford Park."

"Good, we haven't seen him in two months. He stays busy."

"And so will we be in close to seven months," Chastity whispered.

"S-s-seven months, my love? You're expecting?"

Chastity nodded.

Asher kissed her deeply.

Yes, life was beautiful, indeed.

Author's Note #2

THE VARIOUS LAWS I mention in this story concerning custody and guardianship of children have been thoroughly researched. Thankfully, by the latter part of the Victorian era, when this story takes place, women were finally given a legal say over their children's lives in certain circumstances.

Scott's Oyster and Supper Rooms (as it was called in the 1890s) still exists. It is called Scott's of Mayfair today, and it moved from Coventry Street in 1967 to its present location on Mount Street. The original building's façade still exists. While researching the history, I could not find if they had private dining rooms, so I added it to my narrative.

Characters of mine mentioned in this story:

Harrison Hornsby, Duke of Gransford. You can find his story in *The Marquess of Secrets* (The Hornsby Brothers #3)

Aidan Wollstonecraft, Earl of Carnstone. You can find his story in *Love with a Notorious Rake* (Men of Wollstonecraft Hall #3)

Author Biography

A multi-published author from the East Coast of Canada, Karyn Gerrard loves to write sensual historical and contemporary romances. Tortured heroes are an absolute must.

Karyn's been happily married for a long time to her own hero. His encouragement and loving support keeps her moving forward.

To learn more about Karyn and her books: Visit: http://www.karyngerrard.com/

Also visit her on Facebook, Twitter, Pinterest, Instagram, and Bookbub.

"LOOKING FOR A SWOON-worthy read? You can't go wrong with the lovely and emotional romances from Karyn Gerrard." ~**Vanessa Kelly, USA Today Bestselling author**

"Karyn Gerrard writes very enjoyable, richly textured historical romances." ~**Kate Pearce, New York Times and USA Today Bestselling author**

More Books by Karyn Gerrard

~HISTORICAL~

The Spinster and Mr. Glover (Book #1 Blind Cupid Series)

The Governess and the Beast (Book #2 Blind Cupid Series)

The Copper and the Madam (Book #3 Blind Cupid Series)

Protecting the Duke (The Rakes of St. Regent's Park #1)

The Baron and the Mistress (The Rakes of St. Regent's Park #2)

Knight of Christmas (The Rakes of St. Regent's Park #3)

Bold Seduction (Book #1 Hornsby Brothers Series)

The Vicar's Frozen Heart (Book #2 Hornsby Brothers Series)

Marquess of Secrets (Book #3 Hornsby Brothers Series)

Beloved Monster (Book #1 The Ravenswood Chronicles)

Beloved Beast (Book #2 The Ravenswood Chronicles)

Marriage with a Proper Stranger (Book #1 Men of Wollstonecraft Hall Series)

Scandal with a Sinful Scot (Book #2 Men of Wollstonecraft Hall Series)

Love with a Notorious Rake (Book #3 Men of Wollstonecraft Hall Series)

Duke of Pain (The Rakes of St. Regent's Park #4)

The Not So Perfect Duke (The Rakes of St. Regent's Park #5)

The Viscount of Shadows (The Rakes of St. Regent's Park #6) Coming Soon!

~Contemporary~

My Highlander Cover Model (Heroes of Time Travel Anthology Series #1)

Timeless Heart (Heroes of Time Travel Anthology Series #2)

My Wicked Soul (It's Never too Late for Love Anthology Series #1)

That Christmas Feeling (It's Never too Late for Love Anthology Series #2)

Wild Pitch

He's the Wicked Bad (Wicked Men of Rockland City #1)

His Wicked Celtic Kiss (Wicked Men of Rockland City #2)

His Wicked Cold Heart (Wicked Men of Rockland City #3) coming soon!

Sneak Peek of Knight of Christmas

(The Rakes of St. Regent's Park #3)
By Karyn Gerrard

Prologue

L ondon
    December 1897

Brandon Knight sat across from his friend, Gideon Broyles, the Duke of Watford, in a private dining room in the rear of a gaming club they often frequented.

They were here for one final night about town before Bran left for the southeast coast. The town of Herne Bay, to be exact, is his hometown. A place he had not seen in years.

He had returned to England more than eight months past and landed in London to see to business that should have taken no more than two months to settle. It was early December, and he had procrastinated long enough.

Who would have thought he would make the acquaintance of a duke, much less become friends with him and be invited to join his select group?

They were known in London as The Rakes of St. Regent's Park. Following in Gideon's shadow, Bran had participated in enough carnal adventures to last a lifetime.

Sensibly speaking, he could settle in London, set up his thriving import-shipping concern, and continue with his various salacious escapades until he was too old or too bored, whichever came first.

But he had other plans. A campaign years in the making.

"I've told the others about the new prospects for the Rakes club. Thank you for suggesting Mr. Gregory McFadden," Gideon said. "Another rich businessman to take your place is just the ticket."

"I may return to London sooner than you think," Bran stated as he took a sip of wine. "Thinking logically, why would I stay in Herne Bay? There is nothing there for me."

"No family to speak of?"

"A few cousins. I wasn't close to them before I departed. So why seek them out now? There is no one. Nothing for me but revenge."

Gideon scoffed as he meticulously cut his beefsteak into bite-sized pieces. Age hadn't slowed Gideon, who would be forty next month.

Was this the life Bran wanted? A middle-aged roué moving from one encounter to the next? Taking his meals alone in private clubs?

Bran still needed to decide what he wanted. He couldn't resolve his future life until he settled his past. He at least came to that conclusion. Finally. Which explained his urgent trip to Kent.

"Well? Have you nothing to say about what I revealed earlier?" Bran asked. "I told you of my horrid past and why I am traveling to Herne Bay. What do you think of the matter?" Perhaps he made an error in divulging certain aspects of his past. He considered Gideon a friend, but did the aloof man return the sentiment? When in the past months have they ever had a meaningful conversation?

"You were certainly treated abdominally. But am I surprised? No. Knowing the aristocracy as I do, nothing scandalizes me. I don't know Oakby all that well. The earl often stays in the country. In fact, I cannot recall the last time I saw or spoke to the man. Years, I suspect."

Gideon popped a piece of beef into his mouth, chewed, and swallowed. "Another peer is living near Herne Bay. He was briefly a member of The Rakes before going off to war in '85, or was it earlier? Regardless, his name is Simon Wolstenholme, Baron Stonecliff. I would suggest you look him up to ask about Oakby, but I lost all contact with Simon after he was injured during the war. Married, I hear, despite his many scars, inside and out."

"I appreciate the suggestion, but I'm not interested in anyone in Herne Bay but Oakby."

"Of course, merely a suggestion. Oakby was always secretive. I have heard talk of his wild parties but have never been. I'm not one for those bawdy country revelries that often turn into orgies. That is more Brookton's cup of tea. He might know more about Oakby if you are so inclined."

No.

Bad enough that he revealed part of his horrid past to Gideon, he would not be telling the others in their group. Especially not Damon Cranston, Marquess of Brookton. He was a notorious gossip on top of everything else. Besides, he would only offer a smug comment.

"This stays between us, Gideon. I want no one else to know. Especially any prospective new members."

Gideon dabbed the corner of his mouth with his napkin. "Very well, as you wish. You could have hired Eleanora Galway's investigative agency. She is discreet and efficient and could have discovered pertinent information for you."

How true. Bran had had a similar thought.

Eleanora was Christian Bamford, the Duke of Allenby's fiancée. Once meeting and falling in love with the formidable Eleanora, Christian gave up his membership in their dissolute rake clique. Although Christian socialized with the club for the occasional dinner. In fact, their small wedding would be taking place on Christmas day.

Asher Colborne, Baron Wenlock, had also recently given up his membership except for dinner or cards now and then. The man was disgustingly happy, having just reconciled with a young lady from his past. They were marrying in early spring. Asher wasn't even in London but at his country estate. He would be returning shortly for Christian and Eleanora's wedding.

Bran was glad he would be missing all the nuptials. Sickeningly sentimental affairs, and not for him.

"I thought about hiring The Galway Agency. Not only did they solve Allenby's case, but they assisted Wenlock with his recent drama, whatever it was. It's enough that I know Oakby is currently in residence in Herne Bay. That's all I need to know."

"Revenge is a dish best served cold, as they say. You certainly have had enough time to plan and scheme. How long has it been?" Gideon asked as he sipped his wine.

"Ten years," Bran murmured.

"My God, man. I have no idea what you have planned, nor do I wish to be included in your intrigues. All I know of Oakby is that he is an arrogant arse and not well-liked. But then, that could be said of all in the peerage. It's not that I'm not interested, old chap; it is a case of the less you know, the better. I've got this far without being an accessory after the fact."

Bran chuckled. "I don't plan to murder the bastard or his wretched countess."

"Regardless, send word when you have meted out your vengeance. Will you be returning to Canada?"

Bran frowned. "I don't know, as I haven't thought that far ahead. But I will inform you when I have made a decision."

Gideon refilled their glasses. "I am not one for deeper emotions. They are tedious and interfere with life's pleasures. I'm not demonstrative and seek out companions who feel the same. I consider you a friend, and I cannot claim to have many. Or any at all when it comes to it. So, believe me when I say I empathize with your situation. I wish I had profound advice to offer, but alas, I do not. I am old enough to remember those rare moments of vulnerability."

Gideon met his gaze. "But you, Brandon? The icy veneer has held, and I have a little understanding now of why the ice is there. If I were to examine my past, I would no doubt find a ready explanation for my frostiness."

Gideon paused, a shadow passing his features. As if haunting memories were playing out within his mind. "Keep that icy shield firmly in place, my friend. Do not allow emotions to cloud and hinder your purpose. See to your vengeance, then get on with the rest of your life."

"Have you seen to your retribution?" Bran asked, his voice soft.

"Ah, I've revealed too much. No. I have not seen to any reprisals. Perhaps that is why I haven't moved forward. Don't be like me. Or any of us left in this pathetic group. Do what needs to be done. Show the courage that I lack." Gideon held up his glass. "To retaliation and reformation."

Bran held up his. "Cheers. And despite my icy veneer, as you call it, I also consider you a friend. I will stay in touch, I promise."

Not one for more profound emotion.

That was the problem: Bran felt too much.

He had just learned to hide it well. While he was eager to see this portion of his life closed off for good, another part of him wondered: was he exposing his blackened and shriveled heart to further heartache?

Chapter 1

H*erne Bay, England*
December 1897

Since Brandon Knight was attending the funeral of an English peer, he should not be in an aroused state. Yet, here he was in just such a painful condition.

The cause?

Lady Angeline Hawdon, Countess and widow of the late Lord Nigel Hawdon, Earl of Oakby. Bran's heated gaze had not left her since he'd entered the church.

Bran believed that he would remain unaffected by her presence. After a decade, surely such youthful urges had dissipated long ago? Especially after what was done to him and the countess's role in the twisted scheme?

Apparently not.

Lady Oakby sat on a wooden chair beside the earl's coffin, her back ramrod straight. Her face showed no emotion whatsoever.

A small, insignificant boy stood dutifully at her side, a pale, sickly creature who resembled his debauched father. Bran could see the physical resemblance from his vantage point. His mouth curled with disgust.

Tearing his gaze from the boy, he instead focused on the countess again. A surge of hate tore through Bran, all but killing his erection.

After all these years, that he had any reaction at all to this woman astounded him. He shifted his weight on the ancient wooden pew. It creaked in response. Concentrating on the service could distract him.

The vicar droned on, lie after lie spilling from his lips, exalting the Earl of Oakby and his varied good deeds. The sermon was enough to turn one's bile. It took Bran's self-control not to jump to his feet and call the vicar out on his prevarications. That would certainly liven up the proceedings.

God, he was bored to tears.

The old stone chapel was half empty. Lord Oakby had made more enemies than society or the vicar was willing to acknowledge. The snub gave Bran a slight tug of satisfaction. Good. The earl had been a loathsome creature.

In truth, Oakby had not been universally well-loved or admired. Gideon had been right on that score. Most of the mourners appeared as uninterested as he, or did he observe relief hidden behind the blank expressions?

Bran slapped his kid-leather gloves in his palm as his thoughts drifted to Angeline again.

The first time he'd seen her was ten years ago, as the earl's young bride.

The bride, now a widow, sat stoically at the front of the chapel.

Bran eyed her through half-closed lids. The breathtaking beauty was still visible, but if one looked closely, her eyes were empty and devoid of feeling, her mouth drawn taut, and her face pale.

Part of him was glad she hadn't had an easy life with Oakby.

The vengeful, hardhearted part.

As he impatiently smacked his gloves, his gaze on Angeline remained unshakable. She looked glorious, even encased in black silk bombazine and the long weeping veil of black crepe.

The lace veil was lifted and worn back from her head, framing her face. Was her hair still spun gold, or had it lost its gleaming luster during the past ten years? Hard to tell as her locks were tucked away under the severe-looking shroud.

Seeing Angeline again was more intense than he thought it would be. Her lush figure was one he'd been well-acquainted with, and the curves were still evident beneath the confines of her mourning clothes.

Angeline posing as the grieving widow enticed him more than ever. He desired her, and he would have her.

A bold boast and an altogether strange considering his rancorous feelings and thoughts of revenge. Well, wasn't it said that there was a fine line between desire and disdain? Or was it love and hate? What did it matter?

The organ wheezed and groaned, creating a doleful sound accompanying the morbid proceedings. The small choir began to sing "Peace, Perfect Peace, in This Dark World of Sin."

Bran had to fight back a cynical laugh at the irony. Because Oakby lived in a dark world of sin of his own making.

May the bastard never find peace.

As the draped-in-black coffin was carried outside, Angeline and the boy walked dutifully behind, staring straight ahead. A funeral carriage with six black horses decorated with plumes of feathers awaited the grim procession. Professional mourners stood nearby, eager to be done and collect their fee.

Or so Bran surmised.

The weather was bitterly cold. The horses neighed in annoyance as ice crystals formed around their nostrils. Clouds of frost from their breaths hung heavy in the air.

Bran pulled on his leather gloves, then tugged the wool muffler tighter about his neck and chin. He buttoned his wool coat to keep out the worst of the chill.

No such bloody luck.

Leave it to Oakby to have the bad manners to die three weeks before Christmas and in one of the coldest Decembers in recent history.

The air had been warmer in Canada than it was here. No doubt 1897 would go down as a miserable year for weather. Or so the innkeeper had informed him.

The master of ceremonies assisted Angeline and her son into the carriage. The one which would follow directly behind the coffin.

Bran would *not* be accompanying the procession to the family plot. Oakby was dead.

Now, what in the hell does he do?

Bran had waited far too late to seek his vengeance.

The years had gotten away from him. But how could he have arrived here any sooner? Damn, he should not have lingered in London these past months.

That delay was on him.

Pulling his beaver hat low over his brow, Bran turned and walked in the opposite direction.

He had urgent plans that required his immediate attention.